1
THE CAMEO SERIES

HAPPY BIRTHDAY LARUE

MARCH 8, 1985

WITH LOVE

Art

GRACE LIVINGSTON HILL

Tyndale House
Publishers, Inc.
Wheaton, Illinois

First printing, August 1984

Library of Congress Catalog Card Number 84-50541
ISBN 0-8423-3846-2
Copyright © 1984 by Robert L. Munce Publishing Co.
Printed in the United States of America

CONTENTS

THE
LOVE GIFT

CHAPTER I

*S*HELLS are all very well on a seashore,
with white sand about, and a fresh breeze
blowing; but in this stuffy little room on
the mantelpiece, in a wooden butter dish,
and considered in the light of an ornament—*that* is
too much! Ugh!"

The exclamation was apparently addressed to a
very fat cockroach who stood in the middle of the
room watching the new occupant, perhaps to see
how he was going to like her. So far he had been well
pleased with her appearance. She was small and
slight; and though she had a rather determined
mouth, she looked as though her foot would not be
so very heavy if it should happen to come down upon
his head. She had been in to look at the room in the
morning, had rented it and gone away; and now, just
as the gray, drizzly day was drawing to its close, she
had come back to it, taken off her hat and jacket, and

thrown them on the bed. It must have been his fixed gaze that attracted her attention, for as soon as she had uttered that last word she gathered up her neat traveling dress and started toward him. Her visitor rose up on his hind legs, and pranced off toward the bed, keeping one eye upon her feet all the time, however. She was quick-motioned, and stooped to strike him under the edge of the bed; but by the time her eyes had reached the level of the floor, the cockroach had disappeared from view, and there was nothing to be seen but a stretch of faded ingrain carpet.

She was too weary to continue the search, and so came back to the contemplation of the mantelpiece with its wooden dish of dusty exiles. Over the mantel hung an old engraving of a wooden-faced baby and a prim little girl with one foot under her, sewing. It was framed in black walnut, with a carved leaf at each corner, and the words "Watching Baby" were inscribed beneath. About the wall were its companions, framed in like manner. There was a chalk-faced woman with a low-necked dress and a sheet over the top of her head, gazing up into the sky with a sorrowful expression, called "Meditation." There also was that touching scene named "The Soldier's Farewell," where a stiff man and woman were clasped in each other's arms, with the various other stiff members of the family ranged about them. The girl turned from them in disgust, and with a curling lip which had in it more of weariness than of contempt, began to survey the rest of the room. The bedstead, bureau, and washstand were imitation cherry, and looked brisk and new, as if they could do cheap honors quite gracefully; but the fireplace had been covered with a thick coat of dull, black paint and looked discouraged, while the grate was one-sided, and imparted to the tongs and coal-scuttle a sort of down-in-the-mouth appearance. The table was a rickety old one belonging to another set, and covered with a moth-eaten red cloth with dirty cretonne storks sewed on by way of decoration. There was a cheese box covered with a dark green felt in front of the window, and that was all besides the two chairs and the occupant. There was a sort of despair in her face as she finished the inventory. The room was cheap, and had a good-sized clothes-press, and that was all that could be said in its favor. She tried to remember how much better this was than many a room which she had looked at, and to be thankful for having found this; but visions of a dainty white room furnished luxuriously, with all her precious belongings scattered about it, would come and imprudently contrast themselves with her present surroundings. How would her handsome jewel case look standing on that miserable stork tablecloth? But then she remembered that the elegant thing had been sold with everything else, and that there would be no need for it to associate with low-bred storks. Tears filled her eyes, and she went to the small-paned window to find some other occupation for her thoughts; but there came a knock at the door, and the announcement: "Your trunk has come, Miss; and the man asks, Where will he put it?"

When the trunk was unstrapped, and the man paid and gone, she went back to the window again. The street was quite dark now, and lights glinted about everywhere. She could see the tops of the heads of people as they passed the street lamp in front of the house. The hum and buzz of the wicked, busy city sent a shiver over her. It seemed a hundred times more terrible to hear it through the dark. She went back over her dreadful experience of the past few weeks. It did not seem possible that it had all happened to her, and she did not feel as if she could bear it. Perhaps it was a dreadful dream, and she would wake up tomorrow morning and find it past, and herself back in her own pretty room, with the door open into her mother's, and all her bright hopes hers again. But such could never be, and she must go on and bear her sorrow always. She turned and went in search of the slouchy Irish girl, to petition for a lamp, as there seemed to be no gas in the room.

Her story was like many she had read; but she had thought it could not happen to her—the sudden death of her mother, and shortly after that of her father; then the discovery that the money, which they had thought almost unlimited, was swept away, and that even the home must be given up. A familiar story, yet new and terrible to each one who passes through it. When she found that she must do something to earn her own living, she would have none of the ways that other girls in her position and with her accomplishments would have chosen.

"No," she said to a friend who tried to reason with her; "I can't do any of those things well enough, and I don't like to do them. Besides, places of that sort are full to overflowing already. If I knew how to cook

I would find a place as housekeeper somewhere; but I don't. I can't do anything *well* but trim hats and bonnets!"

And trim hats and bonnets she would, despite all that could be said. She had done it for herself and her friends for years, and had always been said to have good taste. No one could place a feather or a bit of lace more gracefully.

Neither would she stay among her acquaintances and do her work; for she had found that in the general loss of home and money she had lost also some friends who had been counted as her very nearest and dearest. There was a pain in her heart to be fought with, and she longed to get away from everything familiar, and so had come to this strange city, rented a small store on a not very pretentious street, and with a little money that was saved from the wreck she would buy a small stock, and try her hand at millinery. A "cheap milliner," she told herself; for of course she could not hope to get the patronage of wealthy people at first.

This was her first night in her new home. She had had a long, weary day of store and room hunting, and before her were much work and worry before she could feel that she was really started. Life looked very hard to her that night.

"I hope yez won't be troubled much wid the roaches," said the woman who presided over the lamps, as she handed her a dripping, leering one.

"I thought there must be some reason for the cheapness," thought the weary girl as she dragged herself and her wicked lamp up the two flights of stairs. She opened the door, and lo! they had come to meet her—a whole army of them, great and small! They vanished from her in all directions, like the rays of light from the sun. She stood still in amazed disgust. She did not even attempt to catch one of them. So many cockroaches were more than her drooping spirits felt able to face at once. They all disappeared mysteriously in a moment, and left her the room. She looked toward the closet door tremblingly. Who knew how many generations of these horrid, shiny things were hidden behind its grim boards? Would they, *could* they, come out and crawl over her when she was asleep? This thought was too much. She put the lamp on the rickety table, closed the door, threw herself on the not overclean bed, and cried. So a great roach found her when he ventured to thrust his nose out under the closet door toward morning, to see why the lamp burned so long; but he dared not call out his tribe that night.

It was a bright Sunday morning's sun that peeped in and woke her a few hours later. She went drearily to church because she could not bear to spend the morning alone in that room; but she sat in a very back seat, and let the minister's sermon float over her head, as if it were something that must be gone through with, while she entertained bitter thoughts. She was glad when the long service was ended.

The people in the dismal little boarding-house across the way where she took her meals were tiresome, and so different from those by whom she was usually surrounded! She rushed back to her room from dinner as soon as possible, refusing the invitation to remain in the parlor and sing with the other boarders, so haughtily, that Miss Bangs, who gave it, walked back to the piano with a face the color of her old rose dress. She slept some, and unpacked some, and thought a great deal; and at last the day was gone. It was a great relief to think that she could go to work in the morning.

She really enjoyed buying her stock, tiresome though it was. She went from one wholesale store to another, and would take nothing but what was pretty or tasteful, though many a clerk assured her that certain articles were "just the craze," and would sell better than those she had chosen. She preferred good taste even to having "the correct thing," and remained firm.

"If I'm going to make bonnets for poor Irish girls, I'll see if I can't elevate their tastes. I just *cannot* put such ugly things together." Thus she told herself as she passed by boxes and boxes of hideous green artificial roses and various nameless imitations of what never grew upon the earth. Cheap things she was obliged to buy, for her purse was limited, and besides, she expected to serve people who would require cheapness; but there were plenty of inexpensive things that were also pretty. And so she spent much time and nerve, and at last had her little store ready for work. Of but one extravagance had she been guilty. She had found in one store a spray of small, white, starry blossoms, set among their fine, fern-like leaves, the whole thing so delicate and unobtrusive, and yet so natural and in such perfect taste, that it seemed to rest her tired eyes, which had all day been filled with gaudy colors and hideous straw shapes. They were fine French flowers, and very expensive. Her conscience and her judgment both rose up in horror; but she firmly put them down, and said to the clerk, "I will take them." Neither would she listen to these aggrieved advisers when she reached her room and they again tried to reason with her.

"There's no telling but I may have some very aristocratic customer, and she will demand such flowers. Anyway, they will help me to do my work. It will be pleasant just to know that they are there. Those wall-eyed daisies that I felt obliged to buy won't be able to hurt my feelings so much if these dainty, lovely things are in front of them." Thus she spoke to her conscience and her judgment, and they gave up in despair.

At last she was established. A neat sign over the door said MILLINERY in large letters, and underneath, a little smaller, "MISS M. L. HATHAWAY." She disliked the sign. It sounded stiff and far away, as if it were someone else who was being talked about, and not herself, Marion Hathaway. But of course she did not want to put that name out in the street for everyone to see.

It was just in the beginning of the spring season, and customers began to come in. The dainty hats and bonnets that Marion had trimmed and placed in the window attracted much attention, they were so tasteful and unique. The orders came in so fast that she found she could not do everything herself, and must have someone to wait upon customers. She put

a little sign in the window, "Girl wanted"; and there
followed a procession of girls of various kinds, not
one of them satisfactory to the fastidious milliner. At
last, growing desperate, she resolved to hire the
next girl that came in, good, bad, or indifferent. It
was not more than five minutes afterward when in
walked Miss Maria Bates. She wore very big sleeves,
arranged her hair in a yellow knob at the back of her
head, with two little stiff curls sticking out in the
center, and a frizzle of bangs in front, and chewed
gum vigorously. Marion's heart sank when she saw
her; but she remembered her resolve, and engaged
her. She gave the new clerk careful instructions as
to her duties, and Miss Bates smilingly chewed the
while. Marion later wondered if she chewed gum all
night, for she never seemed to stop in the daytime.
The young milliner sat behind a calico curtain and
trimmed, establishing her new apprentice behind the
counter. Whenever a customer entered the store,
she arose, laid her hands upon the counter, and
chewing, awaited a word from the incomer.

It was on that same first Sunday of Marion's stay in
the strange city that the young minister of Bethany
Mission proudly led up the aisle for the first time a
woman who to him was the most beautiful woman in
all the world. It was her first Sunday in this city, and
he took great joy in having her there and escorting
her to church. It was only his old mother. You
wouldn't have thought her beautiful. Her face was
wrinkled, her hair was thin, and her bonnet looked
very odd indeed. But her son did not think so. He

had been in the city for years himself, and had seen fashionable women by the score, but it never occurred to him that his mother's dress was not all that it should be. He had not noticed that it was unlike others; and if he had, he would have thought her dress belonged distinctively to *his mother*, and suited her.

To be sure, she knew better herself, even though she had spent most of her life in the country. She had sighed, perhaps, over the faded shawl and wrinkled bonnet strings that had done duty for many years, and wished, down in her secret heart, that she might have some new things with which to make her advent in the city. But she knew that it was impossible. Even the money for her ticket had been hard to spare, and the salary from that struggling mission church was small. All this she knew; but she was not well versed in the fashions, and did not know that besides being old and faded, her bonnet was of a shape which looked, even to the members of that rough mission, odd, to say the least. They were city heathen, and knew what the fashions were, whatever else they did not know. It was plain that they expected better things of the minister's mother.

The young man proudly seated his mother and went to the platform. He bent his head in prayer a moment, and there was a note in it of tenderest thankfulness that at last he had his dear mother with him. When he raised his head he glanced again at the sweet, peaceful face sitting down in front of him. There were no wrinkles nor faded bonnet strings there for him. He saw only the happy light in the eyes he loved so well, and it seemed to help him. But he heard a titter; low it was, but unmistakably a titter. Just back of his mother sat two young women. They were dressed in some bright figured stuff, with large hats covered with gaudy flowers, and they were looking through their thicket of frizzed bangs straight at the big old bonnet ahead of them, and nudging each other. The young minister saw it, and wondered what it was about. He looked at his mother's bonnet, and at her. The ugly titter had brought a frown to his brow; but a glance at his mother's peaceful face, looking up at him so proudly, cleared it away, and he turned to the service with a thankful heart.

But when the sermon was ended and the last hymn was being sung, a shadow began to steal over his heart, and he wondered what was its cause. Some unpleasant memory seemed to be stirring. He glanced about the church, and his eye lighted upon those two girls again. Ah! he knew now what it was! A foolish thing, indeed, and not worth troubling over; and yet there lingered a disappointment in his heart that his mother had not inspired in others the admiration he always felt for her. How could one look at that dear beautiful face and laugh?

These reflections tinged the benediction with a little severity. He looked his mother over critically on the way home, all the time trying to decide what it was that the girls had been laughing at. As they met and passed two or three women, he saw them smiling and looking at his mother, and he heard one say in a loud whisper, "Just look at that ridiculous bonnet!"

Then he studied that bonnet! He compared it with all the bonnets he passed, and he began to realize that there was some difference.

"John MacFarlane!" said his mother as they neared the dingy house which contained the small rooms they called home, "that was a good sermon. You preach like your father, my dear. The blessing of the Lord be upon your work!" The mother beamed proudly up at her tall son.

And his happy heart forgot her bonnet for a little.

CHAPTER II

It was a pleasant Sunday that this mother and son spent together. She had just arrived a day or two before, and there had been no time until now for one of those long talks that made his boyhood a tender and beautiful memory. There were old friends to be asked after in the country home, and many questions to be answered about his new parish work. Then they read a chapter in the Bible together as they had always done when he was a boy. As the twilight drew on, the mother spoke of his sermon again, and told him much about his father, things of which she had never spoken to him before. John felt as if a benediction had fallen upon him, and he hastened to his evening service with renewed zeal. Nevertheless, as the working days of a new week dawned, he found his heart oppressed with that bonnet! It troubled him all through Monday, and he studied more ladies as they passed on the street. He haunted the windows of fashionable millinery establishments, and tried to find out with his untrained eye what was the matter with his mother's bonnet. He told her once that if she needed any new things she must let him know, and he would give her money; and she thanked him, and thought of her old faded shawl and old bonnet strings, and said she guessed she could get along without anything a while longer. She even went so far as to take out her bonnet after dinner, and smooth out the crumpled strings, and sigh a little; but she put it back shortly into the clean little box where it had lived a long time. Poor old thing! It had done its best. It had seen hard service, and really, in its day, was neat, and even pretty.

What would the dear lady have thought could she at that moment have seen her grave son standing before Madame LeFoy's aristocratic millinery establishment, and looking with a puzzled, troubled expression at a large black tulle hat, rolled up triumphantly at one side, and bearing aloft in its gauzy arms a wealth of marvelous pink roses and buds, their thorny stems hanging gracefully over the edge of the brim? How would his mother look in that thing? He wondered dimly how they kept those flowers so fresh. They certainly must be real ones. He turned to another smaller headdress. It was all of violets, set close together, and bordered with their rich, dark leaves. There was nothing but a strap of purple velvet for strings, and he wondered how they tied it. He walked to the other window. There was

a silver gray bonnet with a sparkling tinsel cord for
border, and many twinkling spears of steel oats
gleaming among the forest of waving gray plumes
that towered aloft. Everything else was pink and
blue and scarlet. He turned from the window in
despair. None of them would do for his mother.
Other windows he looked in, with similar results, until it grew near the Sunday, and he began to fear for
his sermon. He threw himself into his work then, and
tried to forget the fashions; but he had a nervous
feeling every time he thought of having that bonnet
go to church. It was not that he was ashamed of his
mother! He would have hated himself for such a
feeling. It was that he was so proud of her that he
could not bear to have her appear in something that
to other eyes would hide the loveliness of her dear
face.

When the next Sunday came, Mrs. MacFarlane
was kept at home from service by a heavy cold.
John, coming home alone that noon, was startled to
find that there was a sort of relief in the thought that
he had not had to preach facing that bonnet. He
called himself all sorts of names for caring so much
about a bonnet; but still he knew that it was true,
and he resolved that something should be done about
it the first thing Monday morning. What it was, or
how it was to be done, he would not think now. This
was the Lord's Day, to which belonged no bonnets
of any sort or description. And he put it out of his
mind.

But Monday morning bright and early he had a

consultation with himself. The result was that he resolved to buy a new bonnet himself, and present it to his mother, cost what it might. Some milliner could help him, surely; and he was certain he could tell what would *not* do, although he did not know just what *would*. He took from his wallet a slender roll of bank notes, selected a two-dollar bill, and laid it on the table. He looked at it earnestly a minute or two, and then after some hesitation opened the wallet again and took out another two-dollar bill, adding it to the first. There was no telling what a bonnet might cost. Yes, he could spare that if it was necessary, and he counted the few remaining bills. Then he started on his mission. No minister of the gospel was ever sent on one more perplexing.

He went into the first millinery establishment he came to, which proved to be Madame LeFoy's. A tall, smiling girl advanced toward him, and inquired what she could do for him. He was slightly bewildered. He had never been inside one of these places before, and the hats and bonnets swaying on the wire frames standing about the room seemed to be whirling around him in wild confusion. He felt as if in a moment he would be surrounded and wafted away somewhere in spite of himself. But he looked into the cold, steel eyes above the smiling mouth, and said, quite as though he were accustomed to shopping of this sort, "Could you show me something suitable for an old lady?"

She led him to one of the glass cases nearby, and took from it bonnets of various sizes, shapes, and colors, until the young man felt as if she had captured the rainbow, and was offering it for sale in patches.

"Here is one, just the thing for an old lady. Does she wear blue?" And she held aloft on her hand a small plat of golden-brown straw, faced with delicate blue, and trimmed with rich brown ribbon, and dreamy aigrettes of the same tint of blue.

John looked at it a moment, and then said he did not think she did wear blue.

"Not wear blue? Ah! Then how would a dash of red do? It is being worn very much now by old ladies— dull reds, you know," and she produced a gorgeous arrangement of various shades of dull reds, which John thought was a very large "dash" indeed.

He scowled at it and looked up at the rows of other bonnets for relief; but they shone with scorn at him out of their brilliancy. He put his hands in his pockets and looked down at the red dash thoughtfully.

"Haven't you something—ah, something not quite so—so—bright?" he asked.

"Something more subdued? Oh, certainly! Though I assure you these dull reds are quite the correct thing just now. A great many old ladies are buying them. It gives a youthful look to the face, you know."

John raised his eyes to the ceiling and waited during this speech, until the more subdued bonnet should be forthcoming.

"How would she like black? Here is something sober, though it is quite stylish too."

Black sounded hopeful. He turned to see. His first

impression was that it was a small coal-scuttle with something stuck atop; but, as it came nearer, it winked and blinked hatefully at him, in patterns, from every tiny speck of its small space. The things atop seemed almost demonic in their jumping and dancing, and wicked lights shot out unexpectedly from their perfect blackness. It dazzled his eyes. He did not like it; but what was to be done? How did women get out of millinery stores, anyway, when they were not suited with the wares? But then he remembered that he had come to buy a bonnet, and a bonnet he must have, whether it pleased him or not. A dim thought crossed his mind that this thing was worse than the one it was supposed to supplant; but he decided to vary the monotony by asking the price.

"Twenty-five dollars," said the woman, deftly twirling it about on her fingers, and admiring it through the fringes above her eyes, "and cheap at that. It's *real* cut jet, you know."

No, he didn't know; but it didn't matter. He was appalled.

He managed to keep his face passive, however, and, to the woman, seemed to be considering the bonnet.

"Haven't you something cheaper?" he murmured, half under his breath. He felt as if all those hats and bonnets were so many stylish ladies listening and ready to laugh.

At that moment the door mercifully opened, and the steely eyes of Madame LeFoy were turned in another direction. He blessed inwardly the woman with a green bonnet who entered.

"Bella!" called Madame, "come and show the gentleman those bonnets in the last case on the left-hand side!" and she moved toward the newcomer, with the jet bonnet, twinkling impishly, still in her hand.

Bella came slowly out from the maze of hats and bonnets with an air of "don't care" about her. She led him to the back of the room, opened some glass doors, and took out a bonnet, holding it on her hand, and listlessly gazing out of the opposite window at a pile of packing-boxes in the backyard. She half sat on the little shelf that ran along below the glass, and he stood looking doubtfully at the rusty specimen she had placed before him. It was black, with a heap of feathers, and a few of those impish, jumping, jet things for trimming.

"How much is that?"

He asked the question grimly. What did people do for bonnets, anyway?

The girl brought back her eyes from the boxes, and studied a ticket pinned to one of the strings.

"Seven dollars and a half," she drawled.

He looked at it in dismay, as much as to say, "If *you* cost that, how can I ever find one that I can buy?" The bonnet seemed to lift its feathers with importance at him, but he turned away.

"Is that the cheapest you have?"

"Mis' LeFoy!" called the girl with a nasal twang, "have you got anything cheaper'n this black bonnet here?"

"What, the one with feathers and jet? No!" said Madame.

"It's the cheapest we have," echoed the girl without moving from her seat on the shelf; but she raised her eyes from the boxes and set them upon the young man. He turned and walked out of the store with as much dignity as he could command, feeling all the time that the hats and bonnets were jeering at him. What should he do? He could breathe better now that he was out of the place, and he felt thankful for that; but he was no nearer the desired bonnet, apparently, than he had been a week before.

He paused before several other windows on Fourth Street, and then went on. The ribbons and feathers all seemed to be laughing at him, and he could not bring himself to go into those places. He walked on, scarcely knowing where he went, turning any corner he came to, until he halted before Marion's modest store. It was quieter here, and he could look into the windows without feeling that the passers-by were watching him. These hats did not look so flaunting and foolish as those at Madame LeFoy's. There was one small gray gauze hat on which nestled some tiny moss rosebuds. They looked like the buds that grew on the bush before the dear old farmhouse. He looked at them a moment, enjoying their perfect likeness. Then his eyes rested upon the white flowers which Marion had wrestled with her conscience and her judgment to buy. They were lying against some black net lace, and looked dainty and quiet. He felt immediately that they would fit his mother's face. So small and meek they looked amid their fine moss setting. The young man opened the door without more hesitation, and walked in.

Maria Bates arose with alacrity, and chewed with energy. A young man was at all times an interesting object to her. Young gentlemen customers were rare. This young man was very fine looking; and there was a dignified, high-toned bearing about him that penetrated even the brains under Maria Bates' yellow bangs. But then, her practiced eye noted the shiny look of the black coat he wore, and she decided that he was of no account. Therefore she placed her hands upon the counter, and waited for him to open the conversation. He seemed not anxious to do so, however. The moment his eyes rested upon the smart young curl at the end of the knob on the back of Maria's head, the restful assurance which the white flowers had brought him vanished, and he hardly knew where to begin.

He cleared his throat. It was apparent that the chewer on the other side of the counter did not intend to help him any. He took another step toward her, and cleared his throat again.

"I want to get"—and then he hesitated.

Miss Bates held her jaws midway, and waited for the rest of the sentence. He cleared his throat desperately, and began again, trying to make his voice sound natural.

"I want to get a bonnet!"

His voice sounded ghastly. He realized that he was in a trying position. But he said it, and surely he had a right to buy a bonnet if he paid for it. He looked at Maria in defiance. She slowly started her jaws again before asking, "For yourself?"

Marion, behind her shielding curtain, was sewing

an obstinate feather in place and listening. Suddenly she drove her needle into her thumb, and with a jump which threw Sallie Hogan's new hat under the table, she stood up quickly.

"Maria!" she called in a very determined tone. Maria started, and stopped chewing for several seconds.

"Ma'am!" she answered meekly.

"I want you to take this ribbon up to Barnes & Brainard's, and match it immediately!"

"Can't just now! I've got a customer!" she answered.

"I will attend to the customer! I want the ribbon right away. Go, please, as fast as you can!" Marion said this decidedly, at the same time laying down her thimble and coming out from behind the curtain. Maria reluctantly took her jacket and hat from the nail in the corner, received her directions, and departed, still chewing.

CHAPTER III

Marion turned to the young man, and asked, "Do you wish something trimmed or untrimmed?"

Ah! Here was a new question. How many there were connected with hats and bonnets! He knit his brows over it; and then as a picture floated before him of himself sitting at his study-table trying to trim a bonnet, his face broke into a smile.

"Trimmed, I guess," he answered. "I fear I shouldn't make much of a job at trimming it myself." Then he added more soberly, "I want to give it to her all ready to put on. It's for my mother. She's an old lady—not so very old, either, but she has white hair. I don't know what would be suitable. It seems to me that she would like something"—he hesitated, searching for the new word he had learned at Madame LeFoy's—"subdued," he added triumphantly.

There was no glitter of steel in Marion's eyes. They were brown, and, moreover, seemed to take in what he said, and appreciate it. She thought a moment.

"I do not think I have anything already trimmed that would suit," she answered, "but I think I could get up a bonnet that would please you. Would you like black or gray?"

He remembered the jet coal-scuttle, and was doubtful.

"I don't know, I'm sure!" he said desperately.

"Either would be quiet and suitable," she said; and, stooping to a box under the counter, she selected two bonnets of fine straw, one of gray and one of black. He took them, one in either hand, and looked at them. Was that the way they looked when the trimming was taken off? What remarkably innocent things they were, after all, he thought.

She could have laughed at the funny expression on his face; but she stood quietly waiting, and studying him. She began to wonder what the mother was like. There was something touching in this grave-looking young man buying a bonnet for his mother.

"How would you fix—how would you trim them?" he asked after a moment.

She took some ribbon and lace and a bit of velvet,

and deftly laid them upon the bonnets. He was amazed to see what a difference it made in the hideous shapes.

"Then you might have some small flowers besides," she said.

"Flowers? Yes," he said, recollecting; "I saw some flowers in the window there that I liked very much," and he took two strides forward, and peered helplessly through the muslin curtain that separated the show window from the room. She drew the curtain aside, curious to see what was his taste in flowers. To her pleased surprise he pointed to the one rare spray of delicate blossoms. With a strange feeling she took them up, and placed them first upon one bonnet and then upon the other. He surveyed them with satisfaction.

"Yes; I like those," he said. "I think they would please Mother. They are like some flowers that used to grow in the garden at home."

"Which color do you prefer?" she asked.

"Which do you think would be most suitable?" he answered.

"How old is your mother?" she asked again, smiling. "If you would tell me how she looks I could judge better."

"She is about sixty. Her hair is white—but her face doesn't look old. She isn't very large—I never thought about exactly how she does look—but she has a very sweet, dear face," he answered tenderly, hesitating between the sentences, as if trying conscientiously to paint her portrait.

Marion was touched with his description.

"That's not old!" she said brightly. "I should think she would like the gray better. It is quiet enough for anyone. If she were very old I should choose the black, but for one only sixty I think the gray would be prettier."

He blessed her in his heart for saying that his mother was not old, and mentally compared her to Madame LeFoy. But those thoughts recalled another troublesome question.

"How much are such bonnets?" he suddenly said. "I find that they are much more expensive than I had supposed. Do you ever have anything as low as four dollars?" He tried to ask these questions in a digni-fied manner, but was conscious that it might be a most unheard-of thing he was asking. He would not have dared ask Madame Lefoy; but this milliner was quite a different being, and had taken an interest in his mother. He did not look up until she answered, but kept his eyes on the gray bonnet.

She was thinking. She took up a pencil, and fell to figuring, while John stood looking at the bonnets, and thinking how much better they looked than those on Fourth Street.

"If you had it without any flowers," said Marion at last, looking up, resting her elbow upon the counter and her head upon her hand, "I think I could make it for four dollars."

John was disappointed. He had not thought he could feel so disappointed about a bonnet. He glanced down at the little meek, starry blossoms, and they looked as if they felt sorry for him. Marion saw that he was disappointed, but he did not know it.

He supposed that was a secret between himself and
the flowers, and he answered, "Very well. When can
I get it?"

"I can have it ready by tomorrow morning, and
you might come in any time after nine o'clock and see
if it is what you wish. What is the name, please?" and
she poised her pencil, ready to write it down.

"MacFarlane," he answered, bringing out one of
the Bethany Mission invitation cards.

He breathed a deep sigh as he went out of the
door. How tired he was! What a work it was to buy a
bonnet! How did women stand it two or three times
a year? And then, just as a woman would have done,
he fell to worrying because he could not afford to buy
the flowers. At the first corner he half turned to go
back and ask their price; but his better sense reminded him that he could not afford another dollar,
that it would positively take away from the necessary comforts which he hoped to give his mother,
now that she had come to live with him, and he kept
on toward home.

Marion watched him as he went out of the door,
and then her eye came back to the bonnet and
flowers. She somehow felt strangely sorry about
those flowers. She picked them up, and laid them
gracefully against the soft gray lace. They were
pretty—very pretty. She figured a little more,
shook her head, and then remembering that Barnes
& Brainard's was not far away, and that Maria, with
her inquisitive eyes, would soon be back, she took
the white flowers and returned them to the window;
but as she bent over to place them in just the right

position, they seemed to look up wistfully at her. She studied her figures again, until she heard Maria's step outside, then hastily gathering up the gray bonnet and trimmings, she went to her workroom. But Sallie Hogan's green chip hat remained under the table, while she wrought out a sweet gray bonnet. She wondered to herself why it was that she took such pleasure in this special order, and tried to picture the face that would smile beneath the bonnet; and all the time the flowers troubled her, and she thought how much prettier and more perfect that bonnet would be with them on it. The young man's face, too, haunted her with its disappointed look. It was strange for a young man to care about flowers on a bonnet. He must have a good deal of taste himself, or he never would have noticed the difference. She glanced at his card that lay by her on the table, as she fashioned the gray ribbon into shining loops above the soft, white ruching border. Pastor of a mission chapel! His salary must be small, then! She could afford to be liberal to a poor young minister, and the flowers pleaded once more; but she told herself that she had already given much. She had promised to make the bonnet a great deal cheaper than she would have done for others, or than she could afford to do, either. She jerked her thread through and fastened it. It was her judgment and her conscience against her impulses once more. The gray bonnet was done; but its maker was not pleased with it, and placed it in a dark bandbox, dropping John MacFarlane's card after it, and shutting down the cover tight.

Then she brought out the green chip, and sewed fast. But white flowers hovered in her thoughts. She was disappointed in that gray bonnet. She took it out in the afternoon, and worked a whole hour upon it, and then tried it on, to persuade herself that it was better as it was; but all the time it seemed to lack something. It looked bare on one side. She put two more loops of ribbon in, but that seemed to do no good. After Maria had gone home that night she went to the window and took out the white flowers. She laid them on the bonnet in the vain hope that they would look too much, and take from, rather than add to, its beauty. But the sweet things seemed to nestle among the loops of ribbon as if they were meant for that place, and she fancied that they even smiled approval at her. She put them quickly back in the window, shut the bonnet in its box, turned out the lights, locked the door, and went home.

The faithful cockroaches met her at the door of her room as usual, escorted her in, and then vanished. It tired her already strained nerves to see them; but she was growing used to them. It had become a standing rule with her to shake every dress she took out of the closet until two had dropped out, and then she felt sure there were no more there. There were always two in each dress. She had tried everything to rid her room of them, but all had failed. She had made pills of borax and Indian meal, and daubed them all about, but they only seemed to thrive on that. She dusted everything with powder, and spread pieces of bread with ill-smelling compounds; but most of them remained unscathed, and only a few languid ones crawled out in search of water or medical assistance. She was very tired tonight, and it annoyed her exceedingly to know what a small thing had tired her. She sat down in the hard rocking chair; and conscience and judgment came and confronted her.

"We told you," they said, "that you ought not to buy those flowers. You knew that you could not afford them. You were weak—very weak. You bought them. When we upbraided you, you silenced us on the ground that some rich customer would want them, and now you want to *give* them away to someone you do not know at all, and all because a young man looked disappointed, and because a bonnet that you have made does not suit your extravagant taste!"

In vain did Marion bring up the picture of the mother, and her pleasure in the bonnet, and represent how much better the bonnet would look with those flowers. Judgment was inexorable. She gave up at last and went to bed.

She was in the little room back of the store early the next morning, trying once more to make the gray bonnet look as she thought it should. She was just holding it at arm's length, to discover what was the matter, when she heard the voice of her serving-maid. It was raised from the pleasant drawl she usually used in talking with customers, "Miss Hath'way, how much d'you say these little white flowers was?"

She lifted the curtain slightly, and peered out.

There stood an elegant young lady with the flowers in one hand, waiting for her answer, while Maria was taking a leisurely survey of the customer's wardrobe, and getting pointers for her next shoddy suit. Marion made a sudden resolution, and dropped the curtain quickly.

"They are not for sale," she said quickly. "They are to go on a bonnet that goes out this morning."

Judgment stood appalled, while the young lady laid the flowers down in disgust, and walked out of the store.

"Now see what you have done!" said judgment. "You have lost a patron by that. She was a rich lady too. When you had a good chance to sell those miserable little flowers, you have thrown it away, and are going to *lose* the money you paid for them."

For answer she looked at the small clock on the table, and seeing it was almost the time she had set for the gray bonnet to be inspected, she sent Maria on an errand that was likely to keep her some time. She had no notion of having those eyes watching when the young minister came for the bonnet, nor of having her possibly overhear talk about the price. Maria well out of the way, she took the bonnet out once more, and went for the flowers. Her fingers trembled slightly as she fastened them, but she felt triumphant. Perhaps it was foolish, but it was nice. She was tired having judgment lord it over her. She liked to follow her own sweet will once in a while, and it was nobody's business but her own what she did with those flowers. Since she had bought them against her judgment, why should she not dispose of them without consulting that autocrat? The knob of the store door was turned just as she fastened the last stitch. There was a glow of excitement in her eyes, and her cheeks were slightly flushed. She went out to wait upon the young minister in her store with the same grace which had made her charming in society.

CHAPTER IV

Before she opened the box she explained to him that she had found she was able to make the bonnet and put the flowers on for the price he had mentioned; and then she brought it forth. There was unmistakable delight in John MacFarlane's eyes as he viewed that bonnet. The soft white ruche looked to him just like his mother; and the dainty flowers, settled among the rich folds of gray ribbon, seemed like small Quakeresses. It was quietness itself, and yet he felt with pride that it could hold up its head with any aristocratic bonnet at Madame LeFoy's.

"I like it," he said simply. "I'm so glad for the flowers."

It seemed as if he were thanking her for a favor done as to a personal friend, not at all in a business-like way.

She put the bonnet carefully in its wrappings in the box; and as she did so the flowers seemed to nod to her and say, "You have done right. You will not be sorry."

John, as he proudly paid for his bonnet, thanked her for the help she had given him. He felt almost as happy this morning as when he was a little boy and had a holiday in which to go fishing. That bonnet had troubled him all night, in dreams appearing in various forms, until he had come to fear that his mother never would be able to wear it. He had gone after it this morning very doubtfully. He wished he had never thought of a bonnet, and almost feared to go in and look at it; and, lo! here it was, flowers and all, and prettier than any bonnet he had seen for twenty-five dollars even. How could he help expressing some of his delight?

"I shall tell my mother that you helped about this, and she will be very grateful, I'm sure. I never could have found one if someone hadn't helped me, I'm afraid," he said as he was going out.

It was a strange thing to say to a milliner, perhaps, but he said it. She smiled, and said she was glad to have helped, and she hoped his mother would like the bonnet; and then he was gone, and she went back to her work.

It was lonely with the flowers gone. Perhaps it was foolish, after all, for her to have put them on; but she was glad she had done it, and she wished she could peep in at the window when the bonnet was presented, and see the mother, and hear what was said. She thought of her own mother, and tears gathered in her eyes. She brushed them away. The flowers had somehow started painful thoughts. By and by Maria came back, and chewed and waited on a few customers; and the day wore away until Marion could go back to her dreary little room and her cockroaches.

John MacFarlane carried his white box proudly through the streets. He felt already that he could give a better heart to his next sermon. He looked in at Madame LeFoy's triumphantly as he passed. As he neared home he began to wonder just how he should present his gift, and wished it was Christmas, or that there was a birthday somewhere for an excuse. He began to feel awkward about it, and finally decided to put it away until Saturday evening, when he and his mother were having their after-tea talk. He had trouble getting it out of sight, and changed its hiding place often, lest his mother, in clearing up, should stumble upon it, and spoil his surprise. Then he waited for Saturday evening to arrive with as much impatience as a boy waits for Christmas morning. Two or three times he took the box out and lifted the tissue-paper wrappings to get a peep; and the flowers always smiled up reassuringly. Over his study, his work, and even his pastoral visits, during that week the gray bonnet hovered like a pleasant thought.

The hour came at last; and, her work all done for the week, his mother sat down by the bright student lamp with her knitting. Now was the time. He went to his study, and brought the box from its hiding place.

"Mother, I have a present for you," he tried to say calmly; but in spite of himself there would steal into his tone some of his old boyish eagerness.

"Why, bless you, boy! What have you there?" she said with pleasant inquisitiveness, looking over her glasses at the box, and holding her knitting with both hands.

He untied the cord, pulled aside the wrappings, drew out the bonnet, and held it awkwardly on his hand. There was triumph in his eyes, and pleased surprise in his mother's. Neither of them spoke for a full minute.

John stood with his head a little to one side, taking a back view of the bonnet, and seeing how it would appear to the two gigglers if they should come to church again tomorrow.

And the mother looked at it, and at her handsome son, and then away beyond the bonnet into her past. Tears gathered in her eyes.

"John, dear boy!" she said, and her voice trembled slightly, "your father did just that for me once. You're like your father, John."

The tender tones touched the young man's heart. It pleased him beyond anything to know that he was like his father. He went over to his mother, bent, and kissed her forehead. She put out her hand for the bonnet, and held it off admiringly, then drew it nearer, and smoothed lovingly the shining folds of rich new ribbon. She liked bonnet strings that were not crumpled.

"It's a beautiful bonnet, John. I'm afraid you've been extravagant. I'm nothing but an old woman now, you know, and anything would do for me." But she looked with pleased eyes upon the flowers.

"The dear things!" she said. "They look so like the

little flowers that bloomed in our front yard at home. You don't remember them, I suppose. It seems as if I must smell them," and she bent her head toward them.

John still stood by her, watching, well-satisfied, pleased as any boy at the praise she gave it.

"Mother, tell me about the other bonnet, the one father brought you?" he said with a gentle, questioning intonation.

The tears came to her eyes again, and that far-away, longing look settled over her face.

"It was before we were married, dear," she said. "He had heard me say that I must have a new bonnet; and so one day when he went to the city he remembered it, and brought me one when he came back."

She smiled to herself as she said it, looking off in the shadowy corner of the room. She could almost see her tall young lover standing with the bonnet in his hand, and waiting for her admiration, even as her son had just stood. How it all came back to her—the pleasure they had in trying it on, and the walk in the moonlight afterward! It seemed but a few days ago; and now here was her son, as old as his father had been, and doing the same thing, only the bonnet was not so youthful as the other had been.

"It was a white bonnet, John!" she said, turning back to his face lovingly. "You think your old mother would look odd in a white bonnet now, don't you? Well, so she would, but she looked nice in it then. It was white straw, trimmed with white ribbon, and tied with white strings, and it had a soft white ruching inside, just like this one," she said, touching the lace tenderly, "with a fine, green vine mixed in with it!"

They talked some time about that other bonnet; but by and by came back to the present, and admired the new one again.

"I never should have known what to get, if it hadn't been for that young lady."

"What young lady?" asked his mother with keen interest. Her son had up to now, in her judgment, been almost too indifferent to all womankind except herself.

"Oh, I suppose she was the milliner, though she did not seem like one in the least. Try it on, Mother, and let's see if it is becoming."

Mrs. MacFarlane nervously smoothed down her shining, unrumpled white hair, and taking hold of the bonnet just where the strings were fastened on, raised it to her head, settled it, and looked at her son, still holding the strings with one hand under her chin.

"Why, Mother! It makes you look younger, I declare!" he said. "She said sixty wasn't old. Don't let me hear you calling yourself an old woman. You won't be an old woman these ten years yet. It actually takes some of the tired look out of your eyes. You're the prettiest woman I know of, Mother!" he said, kissing her again. He brought a faint pink to her wrinkled cheek. She looked at her son proudly, as she raised her face to return the kiss.

"You're like your father, John," she said again.

Then there was more talk about the bonnet and the milliner; and Mrs. MacFarlane said she would like to see her and thank her.

That same evening Marion was sitting in her dreary little room, thinking. She was too weary to read or work, and so she sat listlessly, letting her idle thoughts wander where they would. They settled presently upon the gray bonnet and white flowers. She wondered where they were tonight, and if they would go to church tomorrow. Suddenly a strange fancy seized her. She would go to that little mission chapel, and see what sort of a face would appear under the bonnet. She would like to see the flowers doing their appointed work in the world, and know if they fitted their surroundings; and whether, after all, judgment had been right, and she wrong. The new fancy pleased her. It would perhaps be interesting, to see what sort of a sermon that young man would preach. At any rate, it would do no harm, and she meant to go and try it. It would relieve the monotony of the day, and serve to keep the painful thoughts away.

And so it came about that the next morning when John MacFarlane proudly escorted the gray bonnet down the aisle, and seated it in front of the two gaudy gigglers, the maker of the bonnet sat in a back seat and watched them.

She could not catch a glimpse of the face beneath its soft gray framing; but she noticed with relief that the bonnet was set upon the head as it should be, and that the bearing of the woman who wore it was dignified and refined, although her black shawl was a trifle threadbare. The instant she saw it she thought of the beautiful India shawl which had belonged to her mother, and was now packed away in one of her unused trunks. But that was only a passing thought. She turned her eyes to the young man, and noted the pride with which he seated his mother. His face was very grave, and without the slightest tinge of conceit.

She examined the audience critically. They were of all sorts. A few well-to-do; many of them poorly dressed. Some of the children were even ragged. It was the strangest audience she had ever seen gathered in a church. She watched the young minister during the opening exercises, and tried to remember that this grave, dignified man, who seemed to feel so thoroughly at home in the pulpit, was the same one who had been ill at ease, and almost embarrassed, over a bonnet a few days before.

"Their Redeemer is strong; The Lord of hosts is his name: he shall thoroughly plead their cause, that he may give rest to the land, and disquiet the inhabitants of Babylon." That was the text. Marion listened carefully. The words sounded new to her; she did not remember to have ever read them. She watched the faces of some of the children as the preacher described the Redeemer, and fastened the explanation to their wandering minds by telling a simple story. She was interested in the story herself. It was restful to think of something strong. She was tired and lonely, and felt as if she were a captive in a strange land. This was simple preaching. Marion, as she listened, realized as she had never done before, what it would be to have the Lord of hosts for her Redeemer. What rest it would bring to her heart to know that he was pleading her cause! The young minister's hearers could but ask themselves, "Am *I* in the captivity of sin, as those people were captives in Babylon? Is the Lord of hosts *my* Redeemer? Can *I* rest in the belief that he is pleading *my* cause?"

CHAPTER V

Marion was surprised when the sermon was over. It had seemed but a few moments. As she bent her head for the closing prayer, the first words of the text kept ringing in her ears: "Their Redeemer is strong."

She had unconsciously expected to find many things to criticize in this young minister; but as she thought it over during the closing hymn, she found she could remember scarcely anything that he had said. She only knew that she had felt all through her heart what Jesus Christ wanted to do for her if she would let him. He seemed a real person to her. She felt the presence of the great invisible army of the Lord of hosts all about her.

During the general rush that followed the benediction, Marion stood still at her seat to let others by, and avoid getting into the press. She turned, hoping to get a glimpse of the face under that bonnet; for, after all, that had been her object in coming. The white flowers seemed to smile a pleasant greeting to her across the heads of the moving people. The minister came quickly down from the pulpit, leaned across two seats, and whispered a word to his mother; and then they came toward her. She did not realize that they were coming to speak to her until they were very near. Her eyes were upon the peaceful face of the minister's mother. She noted that the bonnet was becoming, and that it fitted exactly the kind of woman she was; and then she forgot to look at the bonnet in her admiration of the perfect happiness of the face beneath.

John MacFarlane stood before her, bowing respectfully.

"My mother has wanted to see you very much," he said, and turned toward the gray bonnet at his shoulder.

Mrs. MacFarlane took both of Marion's hands in her own, and said in her hearty, motherly tone, "I have wanted to see you, dear, and thank you for the help you gave my son. He has told me all about it, and I thought I'd like to tell you that I like it very much."

It was so sweet to Marion to be called "dear" once more by someone, that she utterly lost all her milliner's dignity, and answered with a little of her old girlishness, that she was so glad Mrs. MacFarlane liked it; and she glanced up again at those flowers, that actually seemed to be almost winking at her, modest little Quakeresses though they were, and in a church at that. And then they went out together into the pleasant spring sunshine.

"Oh, isn't this a beautiful Sunday? God must take

delight in making such days for us!" said Mrs. Mac-
Farlane as they came down the steps. "You must be
very glad, dear, when this day comes, and you can
get away for a little while from your store."

Marion's face clouded over.

"Sunday is a dreary day for me," she answered.
"I am alone in the city. There isn't anything pleasant
about a boarding-house Sunday, Mrs. MacFarlane!"
Then she suddenly realized that she was not this
woman's friend, as she had almost felt a moment before, only her milliner.

"All alone!" said the sympathetic voice. "But God
is here. You can enjoy him! A boarding-house must
be a dreary place, though. Is your home far from
here?"

"I have no home now," said Marion sadly. "My
father and mother are gone, and I am the only one
left. I am trying to make this my home; but it is hard
work," and she smiled a pitiful little flicker of a smile
at the kind face bent toward her.

"Now, dear child, is that so? It must be very lonely
for you then, truly. I know what it is to have dear
ones leave me; but I never was left entirely alone,"
and she looked up at her tall son with loving pride.

"I'll tell you what you shall do," she said suddenly,
turning back to Marion. "You shall come home with
us to dinner. We've nothing very nice, to be sure;
but I'd like to have you, and let me play you are at
home for a little while. I'll try to cheer you up a bit.
We haven't known each other very long, but I think
we could be friends. The King's children ought always to be able to get acquainted quickly."

Marion paused at the corner where she turned off toward her boarding-house, and looked down, hesitating, and somewhat embarrassed. A great desire had seized her to accept this invitation. She had been on the point of declining politely; but, glancing at the motherly face, she wavered. She longed to be inside a real home once more.

"Do come!" said the minister. "We would be very glad to have you."

And so, after a little demurring, instead of declining, she turned and walked on with her new friends, horrified judgment berating her all the while.

They talked of the beautiful day, and various other trifling matters of which people speak when they are just feeling their way into an acquaintance with one another. After her first surprise at finding herself in this strange and unexpected situation, Marion began to enjoy it. It was so pleasant to have some friends to talk with once more. They came presently to the sleepy-looking house where the MacFarlanes lived. It was not one whit less dreary looking than the one in which Marion had her room; but there were white curtains at the windows, which gave such a feeling of hominess, that it seemed to her a palace in comparison.

Seated in the little parlor alone a few minutes later, with the soft spring wind blowing in at the open window, swaying the ruffles on the dimity curtains, and fanning her cheeks, she was obliged to admit to herself that she had done a very strange thing, to say the least, in accepting this invitation.

Nevertheless, she was unable to feel at all sorry about it. This room was so cozy and homelike, with its plain furnishing, and air of happy, neat contentment! Mrs. MacFarlane had emerged from her bedroom a few moments before, her black dress enveloped in a large clean apron; and while she pinned it around her ample waist, told Marion to rest, and make herself at home for a few minutes. Then she had gone to the kitchen, and her son had followed her. She could hear their voices now through the unlatched door. By the sound, she judged that the young man was bringing wood, making a fire, and then drawing water, and helping his mother about little things. She shut her eyes, and let the breeze cool her lids. It was so pleasant.

Presently the minister came back. The talk drifted upon books; and she found that they had read many in common. It was a treat to her, this being able to speak of favorite books again with someone who knew them and loved them.

Marion, as she sat down to the small white table, wondered when she had ever been so hungry. There was not so great a variety for dinner, nothing so elaborate as they would have had at her boardinghouse; but everything looked nice. The cold meat, cut into thin, pink slices, and the warmed-up potatoes, had a homelike taste. Homemade bread, too, was a rare treat to her now, and the coffee was just right. She asked about the Mission Chapel and its work, and gained a new idea of city missions. After dinner she would help with the clearing away, though Mrs. MacFarlane said that she could do it

alone, and that Marion was to rest. But she per-
sisted, and then they talked. Marion found that the
mother was fully as intelligent as the son. But it was
after the work was done, and they came back to the
little parlor to sit down and talk, that there came the
most helpful time for Marion. It was a talk that she
remembered all her life afterward with thankfulness.

The minister had gone to his mission chapel, and
they were alone. His mother had coaxed from
Marion, little by little, the story of her sorrows; and
she had told it with trembling lips. The elder woman
had listened sympathetically to it all.

"But, Mrs. MacFarlane," Marion said, looking up
as she finished the recital, "you are mistaken in me
about one thing. I do not want to wear a false character. You said I was one of the children of the King,
and I'm not."

Her head drooped low over the last words, and the
tears gathered in her eyes while she waited for a
reply. It came in a loving, but sorrowful and disappointed tone.

"Not one of the children of the King, dear? Whose
child are you, then?

"Whose am I?" asked Marion, startled and puzzled.

"Yes, dear," said the voice, so tender and sad.
"You must belong to someone. Whose child are you,
if you aren't the King's?"

"Oh, don't!" said the girl, shuddering, and hiding
her face in her hands. "That is dreadful! I never
thought of it so before."

Then she felt a loving arm around her. "Dear child," said the sweet voice again, "you are one of the King's children, even though you have not been serving him. Don't you know he bought you with a price? You are his, only you have been serving someone else, and have not acknowledged your true Father."

It was a long talk they had. Marion's tears flowed fast at first, but gradually she began to see the light. She knelt with Mrs. MacFarlane, and gave herself to Christ, and arose with a new feeling of peace in her heart. Her soul had been reaching out for help for a long time, but she did not know where to go to satisfy the great longings which had filled her. Now she felt that Jesus Christ was going to fill her heart, and that all would be different.

The afternoon went swiftly by, and she had hardly realized that time was passing until she suddenly remembered that it was growing dark, and that the walk home was not a short one. She hastened away, then, but not until they had made her promise to come again.

CHAPTER VI

She thought it all over when she sat alone in her little room that evening. How strange it had been—the bonnet, the flowers, her resolve to go to the chapel, the invitation, and now the wonderful Presence that seemed to fill her heart and overflow into the room! She glanced about. She did not seem to mind the dusty shells with their mockery of the sea, nor the forlorn engravings, nor even the cockroaches. She had something now to be really happy over; and she hummed a little tune as she went about her preparations for rest.

A determination was forming itself in her mind, and it grew stronger as the week progressed. She would go to that little chapel every Sunday. To be sure, it was quite a walk; but what was that? It would do her good. Besides, her only friends in the city were there, and she had found more good there than in any of the other churches she had attended. To be sure, she had not been in the right frame of mind to get good from the other churches; this she realized: but she had a longing after the chapel, and she meant to go. She began to decide that her judgment would have to be reeducated.

It was not long before her new pastor called upon her, and then called again, and brought his mother, who took her in her arms and kissed her, and called her, "My dear," quite as if she were an old friend. It brought a warm glow to Marion's lonely heart to feel that she had such friends, and life looked less dreary to her after that call.

It was only the following Wednesday evening that she was sent for to come down to the dingy parlor of her boarding-house; and there stood Mr. MacFarlane, hat in hand. Would she like to go to the chapel prayer meeting? If so, he would be pleased to have her company. It was so pleasant a walk, and the young minister was so entertaining, that it thoroughly rested her after her day's confining work. Then the prayer meeting was so homelike, and helped her as she had not been helped in many a year. She found herself wondering why she had never been to prayer meetings before. After that John MacFarlane frequently stopped for her on his way to meeting; and it made a bright spot in the midst of the long, busy week for the little milliner.

One afternoon John stepped into the store to bring a note from his mother, begging that Marion would take tea with them that evening. On this occasion Maria was out, and he looked about him at the bonnets, and wondered that he had ever been so afraid of one. He felt himself a connoisseur in bonnets now.

Marion had many pleasant times in the small, cheery parlor of the MacFarlanes. There was a restfulness and peace which she had never found in any of the homes of her fashionable friends. The young minister dropped into the store often to bring these delightful invitations. Now and then he brought a book which he thought would please her. Once or twice he asked her company to a fine lecture or concert; and so, little by little, they grew to be better acquainted.

The busy summer flew by more pleasantly than Marion had imagined it could, and the autumn came on. When the wind began to blow chilling messages from the approaching winter, Marion thought of her mother's shawl, and she looked for several Sundays meditatively at the rather thin black one that Mrs. MacFarlane wore to church. She unpacked hers one day from its camphor wrappings, and shook it out in soft folds upon her bed. Then she sat for a long time with tears in her eyes. Would she, could she, give it up—her mother's shawl? She did not expect to use it herself, it was true. It would hardly be suitable for her. Besides, she had other warm wraps, and did not need it. But would Mrs. MacFarlane accept it? Could she bear to give up the shawl, and see someone else wearing it, when it reminded her so of her dear mother?

"But Mother would be pleased if she knew it. She always gave her beautiful things away. I know she would like it. And Mrs. MacFarlane has been so good to me, and I love her very much," she said to herself.

A few days thereafter the shawl, wrapped in heavy paper, and bearing Mrs. MacFarlane's address, was sent to her by a small brother of Maria Bates, who happened to be playing marbles outside the store. There was a little note accompanying it which touched the dear lady even more than the gift of the shawl had pleased her, which was saying a good deal. She read it through twice, and then with tears in her eyes she said, "Dear child!" and, wiping the moisture from her glasses with the corner of her smooth, white handkerchief, she handed it over to her son:

Dear Mrs. MacFarlane,

You have been so very good to me, and I love you so much, that I want to send you this shawl. It was my dear mother's, and I would like to see you wearing it. I think, too, it would please her. She must love you for having brightened the lonely life of her child. Please accept it as a slight token of the gratitude and love I have for one who has helped to bring peace to my heart.

Yours lovingly,
Marion Hathaway

The shawl was a welcome surprise to Mrs. MacFarlane. She had just been planning to make her thin black one do all winter by folding a smaller thick red one inside it; but even then it would have been thin. Her son was more pleased than he expressed even to his mother. He enjoyed seeing her with the heavy, beautiful shawl around her. It always seemed to him that beautiful things belonged to his mother, though she looked queenly to him in the commonest thing she wore.

It was toward spring again, almost a year from the time when Marion and Mrs. MacFarlane had first come to the city. The postman rang at the MacFarlanes', and handed John, who came to the door, a letter. He glanced at the postmark in feverish haste, then went to his study, and closed the door behind him, tearing open the letter as if it contained some important message. As he read, the anxious, wistful look on his face changed to one of gladness. He half turned to open the door and read it to his mother; but, thinking better of it, reached up to the hook behind his study door for his hat and overcoat.

"I'm going out for a little while, Mother," he said as he passed through the sitting room.

He went with rapid steps down the street, never looking up at the bright-eyed spring bonnets that nodded to him from Madame LeFoy's window. On he went, straight to the little side street where lived his milliner.

"May I come into your work room for a few minutes?" he asked Marion, as she came forward, smiling, to meet him. "I want to talk a little, and I don't want to hinder you. Maria is safe," he said reassuringly, as he saw Marion hesitate, and glance uneasily out of the window. "She has reached only the next corner above here with the bonnet you have sent her home with, and she is talking with a young man. She's likely to stand there some time yet, I should say. How far had she to go?"

"Away over to East Fletcher Street," Marion answered happily. "Come in. I wouldn't let you, only I'm very busy this morning."

He sat down; she took up her work, and they talked pleasant commonplaces for a minute or two, when he said suddenly, "I have received a call to Springdale!" and handed her the letter which had come that morning.

She started slightly, but took the letter, and read it. The color mounted into her face; but her lips wore their firm little curve, with perhaps more dignity than usual.

"It is a very good salary, and a pleasant field for work, I should think," she said, trying to speak composedly; "but I—" she hesitated, and a flush mounted up into her face. She began again "We shall—" she caught herself once more, the red in her cheeks spreading even to her forehead. She realized that there was no one, unless it were Maria Bates, in connection with whom she might use that pronoun "we."

She resolved this time to gain entire control of herself, and, straightening up a refractory loop of ribbon, began the sentence once more. "Your congregation will miss you very much indeed," she said, this time in a clear, unnatural voice; and then realizing that she had made a decided muddle of things, and feeling vexed over it, she thrust her needle through ribbon and bonnet and finger with a force which set every nerve tingling in sympathy with the poor abused finger. When she looked up it was only to find the minister's eyes full upon her, and an amused expression on his face.

"Finish your first sentence, won't you, please?" he asked in a tone that demanded an answer.

She looked down a moment.

"It began with 'I,' " he said, as she still hesitated.

"I shall miss your mother very much indeed," she finished quickly, with a demure air, and went on with her work, though her cheeks were glowing.

Then they both laughed. He recovered his gravity first. Perhaps he realized that Maria Bates' continued absence was uncertain, and his time might be short. He put the letter in his pocket, and drew his chair close to hers.

"Marion," he said, taking both her trembling, cold hands into one of his, and with the other landing the bonnet she was sewing, with all its trimmings, right into the middle of a box of crush roses, "will you go to Springdale with me, and help me begin the new work?"

If Maria Bates had but known what was going on

behind the calico curtain in the little store that morning, she would not have stood smiling and simpering so long on the corner of Second Street with the young man who wore so elegant a paste-diamond scarf-pin. But the world moves on, and waits for none. Even Maria Bates and young Mosely were called, by what they used for a conscience, to move on; and in course of time Maria had finished her errand, and was on the way back.

Marion finally succeeded in impressing this fact upon John MacFarlane; and he discreetly took himself away, just in time to escape Maria's scrutinizing glance, promising, however, to return at six o'clock precisely that evening and take her home to his mother.

"Mother," he said a little after six, as he threw open the parlor door, and stood so that he filled the doorway entirely, "I have a present for you."

"Bless the boy! What is it? Another bonnet?" she asked mischievously, looking at him with a twinkle in her eyes.

"No, it's not a bonnet this time; it's the milliner herself." And he stood aside triumphantly, and gently pushed the blushing Marion in front of him.

Now the cockroaches are looking for a lodger, and the store windows where once smiled the white blossoms are full of candy canes and dogs and cats, with a box of cigars and a few wilted bananas by way of variety; and many ladies who were just beginning to find out Marion's dainty taste are wondering what has become of that elegant little milliner who made such "loves of hats at such ridiculous prices!"

But there is a small white parsonage with green blinds, set in the midst of a wide green lawn which slopes away on the right to a pretty stone church, somewhere. On the porch in pleasant weather sits a lovely old lady, whose hair is crowned by beautiful soft white caps. She knows what has become of the milliner, and so does the minister. And the people who live in the pleasant village streets, and out on the green hills nearby, love her with all their hearts.

"MY BROTHER'S KEEPER"

*T*HREE young men sat together one Sunday afternoon in the reception room of a private boarding-house. The day was rainy and disagreeable, and at least two of the young men looked bored by the state of circumstances. They had read the morning paper through, yawned many times, and made all the remarks about the weather that they could think of. The third young man was a comparative stranger to the others. He was a young fellow with quiet manners and a frank, open face which commanded respect and invited friendship. Both Edward Burton and Charlie Stone felt a desire to know him better as they watched him seat himself by the window with his open book. That pleasant, firm mouth and those wisely merry eyes were interesting. They felt impelled to enter into conversation with him, and each searched his mind for a topic with which to begin. Edward Burton found it first, and began,

"Did you go out to see Bernhardt last evening, Murray?"

"No, I did not."

There seemed to be a quiet putting aside of the subject in the tone of this answer, and Edward was quick enough to see that he had started out on a wrong line; but Charlie was full of enthusiasm the minute the subject was mentioned.

"Oh, didn't you go? That's too bad. You missed it. But perhaps you were there the night before? It's the finest thing of the season."

The mild, quiet eyes were raised again; and the young man replied, "I never attend the theater."

There was none of the "I-am-better-than-thou" tone in this reply. Therefore the young men did not feel as if a bombshell had exploded in their midst, making it desirable to close up the conversation as soon as possible and get out of the room. They rather experienced a feeling of wonder, and perhaps of a sort of envy, at this young acquaintance who could so composedly say that he never took part in what was to them so intense a pleasure, and almost a constant temptation.

"Don't you ever go?" asked Edward. "I know many people do not approve of Bernhardt. I don't much myself. I just thought I'd go once. But there are good theaters, good, helpful plays, instructive, you know, and all that. Don't you go to any theaters?"

"No," was the pleasant answer. "I don't go to any."

"Well, I'm sure I wish you'd tell me why," said

Charlie. "Of course there are bad theaters, but I don't see what that has to do with the good ones. You might as well say you won't read any books at all because there are some bad ones written. That would cut you off from the Bible, don't you see? What's the difference? I've been to some theaters that did me a great deal of good. I have been to theaters all my life, and never got any harm from them that I could see. What's your theory, anyway?"

"My theory is this," answered the young man thus appealed to. "The theater, as an institution, is a bad thing. Its principal actors and actresses are people of known immoral character; the large majority of the plays enacted have at least objectional portions, which is putting it very mildly. If you don't believe that, study up the question and you'll find it so. I have a little book upstairs that you can read if you like. It is called 'Plain Talks About the Theater.' It is by Dr. Herrick Johnson, a man who knows what he is talking about; and it contains some of the most tremendous facts I have ever found. It makes this a solemn question."

"Well, but," said Charlie, who had evidently been waiting impatiently for a chance to speak, "what's that got to do with the good ones? I suppose there are bad ones, but I can't see why that should affect the good ones. I think they are all right. I can't see any harm in going to a theater when it's a good play."

"For one thing," answered young Murray quietly, "the same management that on one, or two, or three nights in the week places upon its stage what is commonly called a good play, the other nights in the week places there something which you could not in decency listen to or observe—"

"Stay away then," interrupted Charlie eagerly. "Don't you see, you'd only be patronizing the good ones, and showing the management that you would only uphold the good ones?" He finished with a triumphant flourish, as if he thought there was nothing left to be said.

"But," said the other, smiling, "your money goes to help along a management that is doing a business of death. What do you suppose it matters to them what you pay them your money for? They are willing you should choose Monday night instead of Tuesday. On Monday night they will take your money, and on Tuesday they will take the money of some poor soul who hasn't your moral sense, who has perhaps seen you enter the same building the evening before, and knowing you to be a Christian, thinks your example one to be followed; and it may be on Tuesday night there is something for him to see that will plant the seeds of eternal death in his soul."

"Oh, well," said Charlie carelessly, "I can't be looking out for everyone else. If I take care of myself and see that I do what is right, I think I'll be doing pretty well. If other people have a mind to go wrong, why, I can't help it."

"Can't you? Oughtn't you to help it?" said the other young man, lifting those quiet gray eyes to look searchingly at him. "What will you do when God asks you, as he asked Cain, 'Where is thy brother?' The Bible says that 'none of us liveth to himself, and no man dieth to himself,' and it tells us that 'we that are strong ought to bear the infirmities of the weak, and not to please ourselves,' and 'Let no man put a stumblingblock or an occasion to fall in his brother's way.' "

"My! You have them right at your tongue's end, haven't you?" exclaimed Charlie admiringly.

But Edward's face was more serious.

"I never realized that there were so many verses of that sort in the Bible. Do you really think it ought to be taken so literally? Haven't the times changed a great deal, and people's views grown broader? If you reason in the way that you have done, that would set up a pretty high standard. Why, we couldn't do a thing without stopping to think whether it was going to hurt someone!" he said.

"Yes," said the young man, "I suppose times have changed some. We have theaters and dancing and card-playing and Sunday observance, and a good many other things of that sort to think about now, instead of the question of eating meat that was offered to idols; but I do not see how that changes the principle. I suppose people's views are growing broader; but I do not see why that gives us any right to broaden the Bible rules. God himself said that the road that led to death was broad, and that many traveled in it; and that the way of life was narrow, and there were few that found it. Keeping in mind what word of his, it seems to me a dangerous thing when we can look ahead of us and see the path growing broad. You and I are supposed to be in the 'strait and narrow way,' I believe." As he said this the look on his face was one of tender, brotherly friendship that made his two companions feel that they were honored by his acquaintance, and that it was their privilege to stand on higher ground than that on which they had been living.

"As to the verses I quoted," he went on, after pausing a moment, "there are scores of them. Listen." And he drew from his inner pocket a small Bible, and turned over the leaves rapidly. " 'It is good neither to eat flesh, nor to drink wine, nor any thing whereby thy brother stumbleth, or is offended, or is made weak.' 'But take heed lest by any means this liberty of yours become a stumblingblock to them that are weak. . . . And through thy knowledge shall the weak brother perish for whom Christ died? But when ye sin so against the brethren, and wound their weak conscience, ye sin against Christ. Wherefore, if meat make my brother to offend, I will eat no flesh while the world standeth, lest I make my brother to offend.' "

Charlie gave a prolonged, sober whistle.

"That's putting it pretty strong, I must admit," he said. "You seem to know all about that book. Wish I knew as much. You ought to be a minister."

"I have been preaching quite a sermon, haven't I?" he said. "Well, you should not have started me off."

"Oh, don't stop!" said Edward. "I'm interested. I've been troubled about the theater sometimes myself. My father didn't approve of it; but he never told me his reasons, and I couldn't see that it ever did me any harm; so I went. But now I can see that for the sake of the influence of the thing perhaps a Christian ought not to go. If that is so—and I'm afraid it is— why, I should be willing to give it up. I want to think a little more about it."

Charlie surveyed his friend with a quick, aston- ished expression; and perhaps there was mingled with the look a new touch of respect. It was some- thing, in his estimation, to be able to give up pleas- ure for a principle. He did not quite understand the motive that prompted it, but he could appreciate the act.

"H'm!" said he at last. "Well, I can't say I'm ready for just that. It would be pretty tough for me to give up going to the theater for the sake of some old fellow down on Scrogg's Lane, if that's where you locate the 'weak brother.' I'd have to think a long time before I made up my mind to that, I'm afraid."

"You are both talking on the theory that it does no harm to you personally to go, aren't you? Now, I don't admit that, quite," said young Murray. "I can't see why you are not harming yourselves every time you pay out your money to an institution that is such a power in degrading the world and pulling down all moral standards. Why is it not an inevitable harm to yourself to allow yourself to become so fascinated with such a thing that you hesitate about giving it up for the sake of some other one? It seems to me that it cannot fail to lead one farther from Christ. It certainly will not help one in the Christian life. Then, too, the majority of even what you call 'good plays' are poor trash as regards literature, and their code of honor is that of the world, and not of Christ's standards, and they hold up for approval deeds that belong to the world—the world from which we are told to come out and be separate."

Edward was looking very thoughtful; but Charlie was ready to change the subject. It was pointing too near home for his comfort.

"What do you think about dancing? I'm not so fond of it myself, but Ed, there, thinks there's nothing like it. Still, I don't see any harm in it."

"I don't dance," answered young Murray promptly.

"Why not?" asked both men in a breath.

"Well, you certainly know that the only possible reason that can be urged against it is the fact that men and women dance together. You know that the world allows liberties in dancing that it does not consider proper under other circumstances. Why is it that you do not walk up to any young lady you may care to, at an evening gathering, and place your arm about her waist, or hold her hand in yours for an indefinite length of time? You don't consider that the proper thing to do. Why is it right in dancing?"

"Oh, but of course we don't approve of public dances where everybody comes!" Edward hastened to say. "We only dance in the best society, at private houses."

"What difference does that make? Are not the men and women in the best society just as subject to temptation as the people who frequent public balls? Why, it is said that some of the most degraded individuals in the world have come from the highest class of society, and many of them, according to their own

confession, have been first led astray through the
fascinations of dancing. Not the mere motion, for
that is good exercise. You must know yourself that
you have often been led to say, or to let your eyes
say, much more than you really meant, when you
were dancing. The touch of the hand, and the eyes so
near to one another—it is so easy to go on, and let
the eyes speak. You call it harmless flirting, perhaps, and laugh about it. But you feel a pleasure in
it that you would not feel if you were dancing with
me, or your sister or your mother. That's my objec-
tion to dancing. And then, even if you personally,
and the ones in the best society with whom you
dance, were exempt from this temptation, there is
the 'weak brother' for you to look out for still. He
cannot dance in the 'best society,' you know, nor in
private houses. He dances with his own society. He
says, 'That Christian dances; why shouldn't I?' "

"My, that weak brother again!" exclaimed Charlie
carelessly. "I should think he would get to be a
terrible nuisance after a while."

"I think perhaps he would," answered the young
man, "if it were not for that added phrase, 'For
whom Christ died.' If he loved him enough to die for
him, I surely ought to be able to give up something
for his sake."

"And cards?" asked Edward.

"It seems to me that is much the same. Of course
you believe it is wrong to gamble. The games that
you play probably do not require that. But there is
the possible danger to yourself of the fascination of
the game, which may lead you into gambling. And

there is the 'weak brother.' He has been led to destruction many and many a time by those bits of pasteboard. You can't tell who about you has an inherited tendency in that direction. The weak brother doesn't always have his name written plainly upon him. He is everywhere. It seems to me that where a thing is known to have danger in it, we had better let it alone. Read Bishop Vincent's little book, *Better Not,* and see if you don't agree with me. If I find a thing that has led many, or any, souls to throw away their chances of eternal life, I think it is a thing for a Christian to keep clear of. It makes pretty solemn business out of life."

The tea-bell broke the silence that followed these words. The afternoon was over. Young Murray felt half sorry that he had said as much as he had done. But he did not know how he could conscientiously have said less.

Charlie Stone was the first to walk out at the door; and as the other two followed him, Edward placed his hand detainingly upon Frank Murray's arm, and said in a low tone, "I thank you for what you have said this afternoon. I have never thought of these things in just that way. I think it will make some difference in my life."

"LIVING
EPISTLES"

OM RUSHMORE was seated in the
evening train, tapping his toe impatiently
as he waited for the signal to start. He
had been detained until this 6:30 train;
and he was in a hurry to be home, for there was
dinner to be eaten, and several little things to attend
to before evening service. He did not really see how
he could spare the time to go to the meeting that
evening, but he had promised that earnest-faced
sister of the new minister that he would come. He
was sorry now that he had done it. It was never wise
to make promises; but now that he had given his
word he must keep it.

Just then, with a burst of rather hilarious laughter, there entered a group of young girls with books
under their arms. They seemed to be bent on some
sort of lark; for their spirits were out of all keeping
with the amount of amusement on hand, so young
Rushmore thought. He turned to look out of the window, thinking no more about them. But here came

more young people with the same kind of books under their arms, and behind them one or two older gentlemen and two ladies, who seemed to belong to the same group!

He looked curiously at the book in the hand of a young man that stood talking just under his window. *"Gospel Hymns No. 6, Christian Endeavor Edition,"* he read. It struck him as rather curious that a company of young people should be boarding the train on a week night, with copies of religious singing books under their arms. Then he remembered that this must be the delegation of Christian Endeavorers that was coming out to Brinton to hold that wonderful meeting that he had promised to attend. Now he would have a chance to study them beforehand, and see whether they were as extraordinary people as he had been led to suppose.

A bevy of young people were on the back platform just behind him. There was a great deal of loud laughter, and some of them seemed to be uproarious. All at once, with an explosion of merriment, a young girl was pushed into the car. She was nicely, stylishly dressed, and had a pretty, refined face, which was hardly in keeping with her actions.

She stumbled up the aisle of the car, calling aloud to her friends: "Come on, Mamie! Let's get the best seats! Here, Charlie, here's a place! Hurry! Quick! before Fred gets here; he'll take everything there is going! Here, Jennie, give me that peanut-bag. You selfish thing! You aren't going to eat them all up, are you?"

The party had turned over a seat opposite Tom

Rushmore; so he had opportunity to watch all that went on without being observed. Indeed, the entire car was treated to their conversation, whether they would or not, the tones were so loud. The young girl that had first come, or rather been pushed, into the car, and who he found was addressed as Fanny, seemed to be a sort of leader among them, though the others very readily followed, and some went farther than she after she had started. She had beautiful teeth, and showed the entire set whenever she laughed, which was nearly all the time. Just as the train started, several belated ones entered the other end of the car.

"Oh, there comes Will at last!" said Miss Fanny, rising in her seat, and waving her handkerchief violently. "I was afraid they'd get left; his sister is always late. Will, come down here! You can sit on the arm of Charlie's seat," she called from one end of the car to the other, in a voice that would have been very sweet if it had not been at so high a pitch, and so loud.

Almost every one in the car but the young man addressed looked around to the young woman that was making so much demonstration; but he was looking for a seat, and neither saw nor heard her, strange to say. She was not to be thus balked in her purpose, with all those people looking at her too. She was not a bold girl, only young and thoughtless; but she walked—or maybe "pranced" would be a better word—up that aisle, took possession of the young man, and escorted him to their "crowd," as she phrased it.

Then the train started; and the merriment, and
peanuts and taffy with which they had provided
themselves without stint, ran high. Some very
slangy jokes reached the ears of the young man
across the aisle, and he curled his lip as he remembered the words of the earnest-faced young woman
that he had heard that morning: "They are very fine
young people that have taken hold of this Christian
Endeavor movement, Mr. Rushmore, and you ought
to be numbered among them. Even if you do not feel
that you can call yourself a Christian, you might become an associate member. I am sure you would
enjoy the social part of it. And I am sure you cannot
be with them long without seeing how much like
Jesus Christ some of them are, and without learning
to want him for your own friend."

Tom Rushmore liked the minister's sister; for one
thing, because she always spoke out plainly what she
had in her mind, instead of trying to honey-coat
everything, and wheedle you into going somewhere
for some other reason than the real one. He liked to
have her say just that to him, to make him feel that,
while he might enjoy the social part of these
meetings, still, that was not the real object of her
asking him to come, after all. It had been that feature of her request that had caused him to promise,
even against his inclination, to go to that meeting.
He had a feeling that she had been fair and square
with him, and that to be the same with her he would
either have to do as she wished, or say plainly, "I
don't want to have anything to do with this society,
and I don't want to learn to love Jesus." This he did

not think it was exactly courteous to say. But he thought of it now, and felt sorry for her, as some sad, wise man might feel sorry for a poor deluded angel that had lost her way. These Christian Endeavorers were not what she thought them, after all. Well, it was just as he had supposed.

Just at this point in his meditations the train slowed up at a station, and the words became distinctly audible again.

The young man called Will was addressing Miss Fanny.

"Say, Fanny! I think you are a pretty hilarious crowd to be going to a religious meeting, aren't you?"

The young girl flushed prettily, and said, "Did you suppose we had to be long-faced just because we belonged to the Christian Endeavor Society? No, indeed! We believe in having a good time, don't we, Mame?"

Then they all giggled.

"Have some more taffy, Will. It's good, isn't it?" went on Fanny. "This is a regular picnic, you know; and we don't have to act as we do at home. It isn't Sunday, either."

"What are you going to do tonight?" asked the young man again, who seemed to wear no badge, and had no singing book.

"Do?" queried Fanny brightly. "We're going down to convert those Brinton people. We're missionaries, don't you know? I think it's just delightful. They say these meetings do ever so much good. Lots of new members will join just on account of our coming out there tonight. Just wait till you've been to the meeting."

"I know one that won't join," murmured Tom Rushmore under his breath, with haughty scorn in his face, as he prepared to leave the train. "However, I've promised to go, and I suppose it will disappoint Miss Bowman if I don't; but they've spoiled the meeting for me. Maybe it isn't fair to judge them all by one or two, though there were a good many of them that were rather ill-behaved; but perhaps they were the associate ones, and haven't got converted yet themselves. I'll go and see."

The merry party trooped down the shaded street of Brinton toward the pretty church situated in a grove of maples, while the young man that had been watching them went on his way home.

"They have grand societies in the city," Miss Bowman had said, "and are doing a great work. Ours is just started, and so of course we have not done much yet; but a few of the most earnest ones from the city are coming out tonight to help us, to interest some of our young people, and to teach them how they do things."

"I'd just as soon my sister wouldn't learn how they do things, if those are Christian Endeavor manners," commented the young man as he thought of her words.

It was a full hour afterward when he walked into the already crowded church, and took a back seat, counting himself favored to get a seat anywhere, as there were already many standing.

Well, certainly the singing was something fine. He must say that in fairness. He had never heard such singing in the Brinton church before. It sounded as if a whole choir of angels had suddenly come down, and were bearing along the voices of the people, and swelling the melody with their own ecstatic music. He felt like joining in himself. Somebody handed him a leaflet with the songs printed on it, and he sang with the rest:

Blessed assurance, Jesus is mine;
O what a foretaste of glory divine!

But that was only singing. Worldlings could sing. He could sing himself when there were plenty of other people with voices.

The pastor of the church was asked to pray; and he did so in earnest words and short. Tom, not being a Christian, did not feel himself called upon to bow his heart in prayer with the rest; and so he spent the time listening to the clear-cut sentences woven together so well, and fraught with so much meaning, and was proud that the Brinton minister could compare with any city minister, even if he did not get so large a salary. In his heart was growing a great liking for this new minister, though not as yet for his calling.

Then the president of the Brinton Christian Endeavor Society, a meek, shy boy, who was almost overcome with his position, managed to speak a few awkward words of welcome, which were responded to in fitting words, well chosen and earnest, spoken by one of the elder young men that had come in another car during the ride from the city. But Tom remembered having seen him behind the others as they came along the platform of the city station.

"Well, he knows his business, and speaks sensibly," said the critic. "But then, he is not very young, and you can see by his face that he is sober minded."

There followed several papers by the chairmen of different committees, giving their experiences in the best ways of working.

"We will hear a little account of the Eighth Street lookout committee. They have been remarkably successful this winter in gathering in new members, especially active members; and I'm sure you'll all be interested in hearing how they did it," said the leader of the meeting. "Their chairman, Mr. Fred Pullman, promised to be here, but was detained at the last moment; but one of their members is here, Miss Fanny Welbourne, and she has kindly consented to tell us all about it."

A young girl rose from the center of the house, from among a bevy of boys and girls. Tom Rushmore thought he saw something familiar about her. She was speaking in a clear, well-modulated voice, which sounded sweet and womanly. He looked again, fascinated at once by the first sentence.

"I think the secret of our success was prayer," she was saying. And just then she turned her head so that Tom saw her full in the face—a sweet, bright face, all full of enthusiasm now. It fairly took his breath away; but there was no doubt about it: this was the same girl that he had seen act in so ill-

mannered a way on the trip. He could scarcely believe his eyes and ears as she went on.

"We meet twice a month for a little prayer-
meeting of our own. Each one of us prays. This was
hard work at first; but we have found that it has
brought us a great blessing to do so. We pray first
for ourselves, and then we pray for the others, the
special ones, you know, that are on our list for
prayer and help. We have to pray first for ourselves,
because we wouldn't be fit to work and pray for the
others if our own hearts were not right. Some of us
think we have come very close to Jesus in this way,
and that he is helping us to do better in our everyday
lives. Then each one of us takes someone to pray for
especially every day, and to work for all we can. And
sometimes this is very hard, when we are asked to
take someone we don't like a bit, and we have to for-
give the person and pray for ourselves a lot before
we can try to do anything for him. We have one
member of our committee who is just lovely. She is
very unselfish, and she is very Christlike. I think she
is the most Christlike person I ever met. She prays
for people all the time; and she never has any trouble
in doing it, because she never hates anyone. I wish
you could have another person just like her here to
put on your lookout committee. If she were only here
tonight, she would tell you more than I can. I'm just
new at this work; but I had to tell you about it, because it has done me so much good, and I thought
you would like to know."

Then she sat down, and there was quite a little stir
all about her as this one and that leaned over to her

with an approving nod or whispered word; and her cheeks were rosy, as if it had been a new experience for her to speak.

Tom Rushmore was amazed. This was a puzzle that he could not unravel. When she began, he had curled his lip in scorn over the idea of that girl's setting up to be "good." Her life did not match her words, he was sure; but as she went on, there was a ring of real earnestness in her tone, which made itself felt in spite of the bad influence of her behavior on the train. Her heedless actions had almost kept one member out of the Christian Endeavor Society, and perhaps out of the church and out of Christ; yet God was allowing her a little chance to undo what evil she had done.

There followed a few moments of prayer, in which many took part, most of them in only one sentence. It was something entirely new and very solemn to Tom Rushmore to hear so many and so young people pray. Something of his old criticism tried to return as he heard and recognized two or three voices that had been loudest on the cars; but something whispered, "They did not know; they did not realize how their actions looked to others. They did no real wrong; it was but your taste they offended. Give them one more chance before you pass judgment on them and on their God, whom they profess to serve and follow."

There was a young girl sitting in a chair in the aisle at the end of young Rushmore's seat. Her face was clear and sweet. There was a wonderful placidity about it, which spoke of a source of joy in her heart.

She was beautiful too, and yet had another beauty than that of mere form and feature and complexion. It seemed that a beautiful spirit was dwelling behind that face. He had watched her several times during the evening, thinking that if he were an artist he would like to paint that face, and yet feeling that there was something in it that could never be painted, and wondering what it was and what made it. While Fanny Welbourne was speaking, the girl's face had lighted up with an eager joy, and she had leaned forward and taken in every word. Now, as they were sitting with bowed heads, from behind her shielding hand came the words, so distinctly that they could be heard all over the room, and yet not spoken in a loud tone, "Dear Jesus, we thank thee for what thou hast done for us. Please teach each one of us what it is we most need, and help us to pray for that."

The meeting closed soon after, and Miss Bowman slipped through the crowd to Tom's side.

"Mr. Rushmore, please wait a moment. I want to introduce you to Mr. Eldridge, the city president. I am sure you will like him."

He bowed assent courteously, and stepped out of the aisle to wait. The young girl that had sat at the end of his seat had also stepped aside to wait for her friends, when up rushed Fanny Welbourne, with her impetuous, eager face all aglow.

"O Faith!" she cried, before she was fairly beside her, "I didn't know you were here, or I never, never would have spoken in all this world. I was so frightened when I found you were here, and could have spoken yourself. But I had to, you know. When he asked me, I just couldn't say no, and have nothing said about that wonderful committee that has done me so much good. And I meant you, dear; you know that I did. You're just the center of our whole committee. I just wish I could tell you the good you have done me." Yes, Tom was not mistaken. There were tears in Fanny's gay black eyes. "And you meant me in your prayer. I know you did, didn't you? I need to be taught what I most need. I wish you would help tell me." Then she turned with a bright smile to the young man Will, and greeted him with some funny remark before the beautiful girl had time to reply.

And Tom, standing where he could not help hearing it all, looked at that pure, sweet face, and felt that here was indeed one of those that Miss Bowman had meant when she spoke of those earnest ones that were following Jesus so closely, and wished he knew her, that he might ask her to pray for him also.

Tom Rushmore went home half decided to join the Brinton Christian Endeavor Society in spite of all he had said against it.

It is so seldom that we are given an opportunity to erase an ill-written page that it behooves us to take heed to our writing, lest someday it bring us pain and shame.

THE
UNKNOWN GOD

CHAPTER I

*T*HE night was cold and dark. A fine mist
was falling, and freezing as it fell, cover-
ing everything with a glare of ice. The
street lamps made vain attempts to light
up their corner of the dark world, only succeeding
in throwing a feeble flicker here and there on the
treacherous pavements, revealing occasional glazed
patches of dirty snow in sheltered corners. Even the
electric lights which flung their brightness into the
night here and there could not give a cheerful air to
the city. The streetcar drivers, muffled from head to
foot, stood solemnly at their posts, as though per-
forming the world's funeral service. Their gaunt
beasts, with not enough spirit left to shiver back at
the chilling atmosphere which infolded their heavy
bodies, strained at their heavy load, and slipped on
the icy stones. All gave one more touch of dreariness
to the scene. It was not a night when one would have
chosen to take a walk for pleasure; and yet one young
man was out with the intention of getting some
amusement if it were possible. He was a stranger in

the city, having drifted there that very day, and for want of money had engaged himself to work in the first position he could find, which happened to be in the shop of a tobacconist. The work was not altogether to his liking. He was capable of better things. But better things did not present themselves, and he needed money, so he tried to make the best of this.

But it was a poor best that he could make out of it so far. He had to go to a boarding-house, and the cheapest he could find was very cheap in comforts as well as name. He was obliged to take a room with another young man, which he did not like. The room looked dirty, too, and this newcomer was used to a clean room. His mother had been his former landlady; and though she was weary and overworked, still she had contrived to keep things tolerably clean, even if it was but a cheap boarding-house, with an air of unmistakable forlornity and poverty about it. Her son had never paid his board, and consequently had been able to attend theaters and entertainments as often as he chose. It had really never occurred to him that he ought to pay his board to his mother. He gave her money now and then, a little, when she was in a tight place and mustered courage to ask for it. But he enjoyed his evenings at the theater, and a young man ought to have amusement. Perhaps it was in consequence of late hours that he had a habit of sleeping late mornings. He was often behind time at the store, which at last drew down upon him the reproaches of his employer. At this he had grown angry, taken his wages, bought a ticket to this city, and here he was. He thought of it all now as he walked slowly along the city street. He was not exactly sorry yet, though things looked very uncomfortable. He had not analyzed the matter, and therefore did not realize that his love of amusement was perhaps at the bottom of the whole trouble. Indeed, he was on his way to find amusement now, though he had not a cent in his pocket with which to buy a ticket into anything. He was not sufficiently familiar with the city to know in what direction to go; but his instincts told him, and he presently found himself in the region of the large theaters.

An unusually bright flood of light attracted his attention to a large building, and he quickened his steps somewhat. Other people were going in the same direction; for, as he neared the corner, he saw a procession of bobbing umbrellas, and people carefully picking their way along the slippery sidewalk. Something very attractive must be going on here, he felt sure. He joined the crowd, and pressed nearer the door. Over the heads of the people he caught a few glimpses of large letters, just a word or two, "Bernhardt" and "La Tosca."

His heart warmed within him. He had seen Bernhardt before, and knew that "La Tosca" was considered one of her very best parts.

"Now, Brad Benedict, this is just your luck," he muttered to himself as he stood back on the steps and let the crowd surge by him. "I wish I hadn't paid for that miserable week's board in advance. I might have found some place where they wouldn't require that."

This young man, Bradley Benedict, as he stood there in the partial darkness scowling at his fate, had anything but an attractive look; and yet, seen in a strong light, his face was not altogether a poor one. He had a good forehead. It would have been called an intellectual forehead if the rest of his face had not been so utterly out of harmony with such a thought. It was not a weak face, but rather an ungoverned, lawless one. A good thought, or sometimes a glance at his mother, had been known to quite alter his expression, until he had almost a look of goodness and beauty. But he had a quick temper and a headstrong will.

By his side stepped an old gentleman, leaning forward in the light, fumbling with some coins, evidently trying to find one of the right value with which to pay for an evening paper he had just bought, and which a small newsboy was holding impatiently up to him. Three ladies, who seemed to belong to the old gentleman, waited a little apart. Suddenly, with a nervous move, the old gentleman dropped his wallet at the feet of the young man, scattering coins this way and that. There was much good nature in young Benedict's make-up, and he instantly stooped to help the old gentleman. But when the wallet was finally righted and the newsboy paid, the old man seemed disturbed, and still searched the dark steps eagerly.

"There's an odd bit of coin missing that I picked up in my travels; I wouldn't lose it for a good deal," he said in a troubled tone.

Bradley began the search once more, and after

some minutes he rescued the coin from a crack into which it had slipped.

The old gentleman's thanks were profuse, and he seemed to be looking the young man over to see if it would do to offer to pay him for the service performed. But Bradley had worn his best clothes when he came off on this expedition to a strange city, and the old man decided that it would not do. Suddenly a new thought struck him.

"Have you a ticket in here, young man?" he asked.

"No," growled Benedict, recalling his misfortune once more.

"Well, I've an extra one that our party won't use. Take it if you want it. Hope you'll enjoy it. I'm obliged to you for your service."

He pressed the ticket into Bradley's hand, and was gone. The young man did not wait long, but followed his benefactor up the steps and into the hall, very much pleased with the change in his fortunes.

He presented his ticket, and was shown to his seat, which proved to be a good one, but not near the seat of the old gentleman. Of that he was glad. He felt more self-respect here, as if he had paid his own way in. He settled himself, and began to look about. The opera house was a fine one, and there was much of interest to be seen; but his attention was almost immediately directed to the stage. It presented a remarkable appearance to the eyes of this young man who was so accustomed to attend the theater. There were seats built up in semi-circular tiers which nearly covered it, and the curtain was raised. What in the world did it mean? While he looked, there filed in several hundred people, musicians with their great instruments and ladies in beautiful dresses, and seated themselves.

It certainly was something new under the sun. He was not aware that Bernhardt performed with any such chorus, but perhaps "La Tosca" introduced new features.

Presently there came in two young women dressed more in the theater style than any of the others, followed by two young men in full evening dress, with another handsome young man a little in the rear. At sight of them the audience broke into applause.

"Who are they?" Benedict ventured to ask the young man at his side.

"The soloists and the leader," replied his neighbor in a tone which made the questioner feel like a green-horn, and resolve to keep his mouth closed.

Above the hum of talk arose the soft murmur and twang of the different instruments as their owners tightened a string here and there. The scene and the sounds were much like the opening of any perform-ance, with the exception of the well-filled stage. He tried to think that there was still another stage be-yond this one, and that presently the curtain, which represented a road winding off to green hills, with lovely woods on either side, would roll up and dis-close it; but he came to the conclusion, after a little study, that this was impossible. He looked the audi-ence over. It was much like the audience of a high-class opera. The boxes near the stage were filled with people, many of them in full dress and ablaze with diamonds. He had heard that Bernhardt drew the elite. He watched the different people as they came in. Some wore quiet dress; but the large majority of those who took seats in the parquet and dress circle carried their wraps in their hands, or thrown loosely about their shoulders, and wore no hats. As he watched, an old lady with white hair drawn into many wearying puffs and crimps, with a long white opera cloak enveloping her stout figure, rolled by him, followed by her footman with most decorous bearing. A man with a tall crush hat, an eyeglass, and a fur-trimmed overcoat reaching from his hat-brim to his toes, followed and made much display in seating himself, and arranging his belongings to his satisfaction.

As young Benedict was absorbed in looking at these (to him) odd specimens of humanity, and making mental comments upon them, there suddenly broke upon his ear a soft, sweet strain, so low and tender that it could scarcely have been distinguished had there not been an instant hush in the audience to let the beautiful music flow over it. He did not remember having ever watched a fine orchestra before. It was very interesting, and to a certain extent the wonderful sweetness of the music thrilled him. He glanced angrily at a group of belated ones in the aisle who were waiting for this to be over that they might be seated, and who were heartless enough to whisper; and it fell sharply upon his ear when some irate individual upon whom the door had been closed rapped loudly several times for admittance. He glared at an usher, and wondered why

such things were not stopped. The music had certainly found a little entrance-way into his soul,
although he was looking for something very much
more to his taste; while this was going on, he wanted
to hear it.

He drew a long breath as the music died away.
Music never made him feel so strange before, and he
did not understand it.

There was a moment's pause, during which people
rustled into seats, and then a rich, sweet tenor sang
clear and distinct the words: "Comfort ye my people,
saith your God." In all his experience of operas and
theaters Bradley Benedict had never heard one that
commenced in this way. He wished he knew the idea
of this "La Tosca." Could it be that it was a religious
play? No; for he had heard it spoken of in anything
but a reverent tone.

CHAPTER II

Perhaps there was sarcasm behind it all. Maybe the
curtain would rise in a moment, and a great chorus
would break in above this sweet voice, and drown it,
and there would be cheers and laughter and something jolly. But this thought grated. He did not want
the sweet voice stopped. Something in these words
appealed to him. They were so distinctly spoken that
he could not but understand; and yet, though he
heard, his mind took in but that first sentence of the
solo: "Comfort ye my people, saith your God."

Comfort. He knew what that meant. He dimly remembered how in his little boyhood, when he fell or

hurt his finger, his mother would drop everything and gather him up in her arms, and say, "Mother will comfort you." He suddenly felt how utterly desolate he was here in this strange city, and that he would like to be a little boy again, with his mother to comfort him. To be sure, it was long years since that mother had had time or strength to think of comforting her son; and if she had, she would about as soon have thought of offering comfort to the president of the United States as to him, for she would not have expected it to be received with anything but scorn. But the grown-up boy dimly remembered the comfort and shelter of those arms long ago, and had a faint desire to feel them about him once more.

"Comfort my people, *saith your God,*" the song rang on. Did God care to comfort people? What would be such comfort if a mother's were so good? What was God? It was a new picture to this darkened mind, the picture of a God comforting beloved people; and the outlines were dim for the reason that there was too much brightness in it for these eyes so long unused to the light.

"Every valley shall be exalted, and every mountain and hill made low, the crooked straight, and the rough places plain," sang on the same voice; and Bradley did not understand it. He looked for the curtain to rise and explain all; but, instead, the chorus rose, and burst forth in one grand prophetic strain: "And the glory of the Lord shall be revealed, and all flesh shall see it together; for the mouth of the Lord hath spoken it." The singers took up the sentence, and shouted it back and forth at one another with a gladness in their voices that made this one listener feel that they were speaking of something which brought them pleasure; and in some way there was a little thrill of satisfaction in his own heart, so used to respond with emotion to what was put before him in song, or act, or story. This certainly was a different theater. A deep bass voice now took up the song in solemn accents:

"Thus saith the Lord of hosts. Yet once a little while, and I will shake the heavens and the earth, and the sea and the dry land, and I will shake all nations. . . . The Lord whom ye seek shall suddenly come to his temple, even the messenger of the covenant, whom ye delight in."

Could it be that these people were going to dare to produce all this in scenery and acting? Would they try to have an earthquake and a storm at sea? Would they try to represent the coming of the Lord? This young man was shocked at the thought. His idea of God had never been a very definite one. He had been to Sunday school when he was a small boy; but the teacher had been one who did not approve of trying to teach much of sacred things to little children, so he had a general idea that he must be good, or a great and terrible Being would do something awful to him. When he graduated from this class, the teacher required him to learn a lesson, and he thought it stupid, so he stayed away. His mother, poor thing, had not known much of God, or at least had not tried to teach him. He had heard God's name mostly taken in vain; indeed, he had not been altogether careful of using it himself upon occasion. Why should he? It meant little to him. And yet, the thought that this terrible song about the Lord's sudden coming was about to be represented, jarred him—frightened him, perhaps. He looked about upon the audience, to see if any one felt as he did; but they all looked calm. One lady was intently studying the scrap of a butterfly bonnet on the head of her neighbor in front; and the eyeglass man had his neck twisted to get a better view of someone in a private box, through his opera glasses. Bradley wondered vaguely how they could be so indifferent. Did people know what this was to be? He had heard that many people objected to the play of "La Tosca"; and perhaps it was as he feared. But the grand voice went calmly on, speaking the terrible words:

"But who may abide the day of his coming; and who shall stand when he appeareth? For he is like a refiner's fire."

Bradley heard no more for some time. His heart was stirred wonderfully. This was awful. He wished the old man on the street had not dropped his wallet, nor given him the ticket. He wished he was out in the cold and sleet this very minute. He would get out of this. It was a terrible place; how people stood it he did not understand. But everything was still, everyone listening. He did not want to make a stir, and draw all eyes to himself. Perhaps when this solo was finished there would be a pause, when he could get out. Meantime, he tried to stop his ears from hearing these terrible words. Nevertheless, they sounded all the clearer in his heart, and he began to wonder how he could stand before this God whom he knew not.

The young man, his neighbor, looked at him curiously as he wriggled uneasily in his seat, glancing back toward the door, and a good woman at his other side offered him her fan; but his discomfort grew. He looked down at his boots, trying to forget the hall, and all about him; think of what he would do on the morrow; lay plans for his future career. And the people in the hall seemed to silently troop away for a while, the seats seemed to be empty, and left him alone with the voice; and swiftly there gathered about him, in shadowy forms, the acts of his past life, and looked down upon him trembling, as the voice died away in the words: "For he is like a refiner's fire."

The contralto had taken up the song; but the change of voice did not arrest the attention of the young man. He seemed under a spell. He heard none of the words of the solo except the closing—so soft and sweet that it fell like a blessing on the hushed roof: "Emmanuel, God with us." It left a tender touch in the air as it died away. There was gladness almost too deep for utterance in the voice of the singer; and yet this must be the God about whom the question had been asked: "Who shall stand when he appeareth?"

There were some, then, to whom the thought: "God with us," brought nothing but wonderful joy! What a God was this!

The joyous-voiced chorus took up the strain: "O

thou that tellest good tidings to Zion, get thee up into the high mountain."

Bradley looked up; the shadows slunk behind, and the audience was there again. It was impossible not to be lifted up by this burst of joy and melody, though the young man did not understand in the least what it all was about. There seemed no sense or connection; and yet he dimly perceived the story running through the whole, as one who listens to a tale in an unknown tongue, and understanding not one single connected sentence, will yet catch at the sense from the speaker's voice or motions, or from the lighting of the eyes, so subtle are the ways that spirits have of communicating thoughts to one another.

"Arise, shine, for thy light has come, and the glory of the Lord is risen upon thee." And this listener felt his soul try to rise and be glad with the rest; but the bonds of its ignorance and blindness were so great that it sank back again in despair. He felt the cold, chill shadows creep over the earth, and darkness so dense it could be felt hiding every face, as the bass told the story. Then gradually there lifted a corner of this heavy blackness, and a little light crept into the sky as the voice went on: "The people that walked in darkness have seen a great light." And there came an eager anxiety in his heart to see that light, and stand in the full rays of its brightest glory, even as he had sometimes longed to be the great, rich, successful hero of some play to which he had listened for an evening, only there was something different about this feeling that swayed him.

It was so dim and indefinite and far away, and only part of him seemed to long for this, while the other part of himself was angry and irritated at the thought, and wished to get away. Why didn't he go? But the chorus was rising again. He would go as soon as they were through; the room was too still now.

Softly as an angel might have sung above a sleeping baby, the music began. The great company of sopranos hushed their sweet notes till they sounded far away in the clouds; then coming nearer, tenderly, exultantly, yet as if there might be tears in the voices—tears of joy—came the words: "For unto us a child is born."

And the basses took it up in the same faraway tone, as though it floated from an upper world almost: "Unto us a son is given."

Still a third time the altos sang the strain, and a fourth the tenors took it up. They were all glad; and was this poor, bound soul of his to have no part in the joy? And what was it all about? A child born! A son given! And why should they all care about that?

"And the government shall be upon his shoulder; and his name—shall be call—ed"—sang the whole company, and then paused an instant for the orchestra to catch up, and gather strength to bring out the words that followed—wonderful words, like great, polished precious stones of many colors and greatest brilliancy, which shone in the setting of this golden music as if placed there by a master workman.

"Wonderful!"

Bradley Benedict sat up straight, his hands

clinched, and his breath scarcely coming through his tightly closed lips. He had never heard a word spoken or sung like that before.

"Counselor!"

A great wave seemed to sweep over him, and roll away, leaving him breathless.

"The mighty God!"

Every syllable seemed to strike a great blow at his heart, and go through him, and a fear came stealing over it. But there was something like a benediction in the next: "The everlasting Father!"

Now, in spite of fear, there came a longing for his mother again. He did not remember his father's love.

"The Prince of peace!" sang the great company, who seemed to have been coming on and on, until now they were here in their full power; and the chorus sat down amid loud applause. The noise of it seemed harsh and out of place to the heart that had just been so stirred by the grandeur of the music. He wished the people had kept still.

And now the orchestra broke away as though the heavenly company had just come down to sing this one song, and announce to earth this one great thing, and were hastening back to join the praise in heaven.

Very sweet the strains were, and Bradley listened as he had never listened to any music in his life before. He did not know it was called a pastoral symphony, and would not have known what that was if he had been told. He only knew he liked it, and was annoyed extremely when a lady behind him sneezed a funny little catlike sneeze just in the midst of it, which set two young girls in the row in front to giggling.

This music seemed to have in it suggestions of all that had been left out of his life—clear skies, and sunny days, and the hushed, sweet peace of green fields far away from city life. He had never known that he cared for these things, but now they stood like beautiful, inviting pictures. He could even hear the murmur of the night wind as it whispered among tall branches, and softly touched tired grass and sleeping flowers, humming a little in tune with a twinkling brook which wound about not far away. The birds seemed all asleep; he thought he heard one twitter as he stirred. The world, the noisy world, seemed a long way off from this quiet place, where all were waiting for some great thing to happen. The meadows were not all alone with the birds. He, Bradley Benedict, the new hand at rolling tobacco, was there. He was awfully conscious of his own presence in that holy place the music was picturing. There were others waiting too. Indeed, he was not sure if the whole world were not waiting with him to see what would happen.

Now the soprano was singing in simple, clear recitative about the shepherds abiding in the fields, keeping watch over their flocks by night. Bradley could see the night sky, with its dotting of stars, and the glory that suddenly shone; could see the angel when he came, and the shepherds' faces. The story was all very new to him. Scarce any inkling of it had ever reached his brain before. Christmas had not brought its revelation to him as to many others. His childish idea of that day had been measured by the amount of property he acquired in sticks of candy, sleds, and balls.

When the tender air of "He shall feed his flock like a shepherd" floated through the room, there was something so infinitely lovely and loving in this One described, that his heart went out in longing in spite of himself; and when the soprano took up the song, with "Come unto him, all ye that labor and are heavy laden, and he will give you rest," there were almost tears in his eyes; he could scarcely control himself, and he had a strong conviction that if that One about whom they were singing stood up there where he could see him, inviting him, he would have to go. He would not be strong enough to resist.

The intermissioin had come. The young leader turned, bowing to the audience, then sank into his chair, throwing back his hair, and wiping his forehead with his handkerchief. Benedict might leave now. Why did he not take this opportunity? Others were going out. The fat old lady with the white head and white cloak was lumbering out, with her dignified footman gravely following, bearing robes and shawls. She looked bored. The young man had lost his desire to get out; but half mechanically he reached down for his hat, until a remark of a pretty girl nearby attracted his attention to the leader.

"He looks awfully tired, doesn't he? My! He must be smart to have drilled them so well."

"Yes; and he's so graceful," murmured her companion. "But it's a dreadfully long program, I think. He ought to leave out some."

Bradley's eyes went to the leader, who looked not much older than himself. The face was noble, pure, and intellectual. He could but admire it. What was this young man?

Why did he give such a strange performance? Bradley had long ago made up his mind that Sarah Bernhardt would not appear this evening. He had made some mistake. But what *was* this to which he had come? Did this young man feel and believe all the singing he had been leading? Or was it mere poetry? No, Bradley decided that it was something higher than mere sentiment. He made up his mind that the young man felt the joy of belonging to that everlasting Father. If he did not, how could he have made those people sing it with such triumphant voices, as if they were the angels themselves, come down to tell the story?

But the intermission was over, and he had not gone yet, albeit his hat was in his hand.

The chorus had begun once more.

"Behold the Lamb of God, that taketh away the sins of the world."

He began to long to have his own sins taken away, and wonder how it could be done; and when the sad contralto voice began to sing he listened eagerly.

"He was despised and rejected of men; a man of sorrows, and acquainted with grief." And then the chorus: "Surely he hath borne our griefs, and carried our sorrows. He was wounded for our transgressions; he was bruised for our iniquities: the chastisement of our peace was upon him, and with his stripes we are healed. All we like sheep have gone astray."

"Have gone astray," echoed the alto, and bass and tenor answered, too, "We have gone astray; we have turned every one to his own way."

"Yes; we have turned every one to his own way," answered the listening heart that now thought of it for the first time. He had turned to his own way when he left his old employer and his mother, and came off here to this strange city to seek his fortune, which was proving so hard to find. He began to see many other things he had done and left undone. How *he* had turned to his own way.

"And the Lord hath laid on him the iniquity of us all."

There was something almost terrible in the sweetness of this concluding sentence. What claim had he upon the great Lord that his iniquity should be laid upon him? During the first part he had been terrified and discomfited because, in the light of the prophecies, he had been made to see his own heart more clearly than he had ever seen it before; and now, when his own worthlessness and sin stood out so blackly, here was a pitying One ready to take the whole. He began to understand the story better, which at first had seemed so utterly incomprehensible. But what was this the tenor was singing?

"Thy rebuke hath broken his heart. He is full of heaviness. He looked for some to have pity on him, but there was no man, neither found he any to comfort him. Behold, and see if there be any sorrow like unto his sorrow."

He bowed his head in his hands, regardless of the curious and scornful neighbor. What did it mean?

There must be love to make such sorrow, and all for him—that is, for the world, and he realized that he was included. Could it be that there was in the heart of this young man at that moment a little thrill of real love for the unknown God who had borne sorrow for him, and with none to comfort him? With none to comfort him! Again that strange little thrill in his heart! Here was a link between himself and this God. Had he not longed for comfort that very night? His mind went back to the first words of the evening: "Comfort ye my people, saith your God." God who had been without comfort or pity in his own great sorrow, yet wanted the people who had caused this sorrow to be comforted! It was *wonderful*. It was not strange that that word, one of his names, had rung out so clear and strong and bright in the music. "Wonderful!" Such a God as this was indeed wonderful!

When he raised his head again, the chorus was singing: "Lift up your heads, O ye gates, and be ye lifted up, ye everlasting doors, and the King of glory shall come in."

And the great question which seemed to be asked by many of all nations and ages, "Who is the King of glory?" was the same question he had asked himself at the beginning of the evening. Who was this God? The answer swelled and soared as from millions of voices besides those belonging to the visible chorus on the platform: "The Lord strong and mighty, the Lord mighty in battle. The Lord of hosts, he is the King of glory."

Some little idea of the power and majesty meant

to be conveyed by these words entered this newly aroused mind, and he pondered over the thought that such a mighty God should care for him.

He was absorbed in this idea for some time, and did not take in what followed, until suddenly, with one accord, quietly and respectfully, the whole audience rose to their feet! Benedict got up too, just as the first great "hallelujah" of that magnificent chorus burst upon his ears. Astonished at all that had gone before, worn out with the unusual emotions that had been swelling within his heart, trembling from excitement so that he could scarcely stand, he listened as the hallelujahs were flung on every side with prodigal hand, like resplendent rockets in a great celebration; and his heart swelled as the words of adoration were poured forth from those hundreds of trained throats: "King of kings, and Lord of lords! Hallelujah!" and felt that he could never go back to his old life, and be the same again.

He was dimly conscious that there followed this another intermission, during which time a great many of the diamonded and eyeglassed sort rustled out, and their places were quietly and gladly filled from the throng which had paid for standing room at the back of the house.

Of the third part which followed, he remembered only the first solo, that wonderful sentence, the climax of our trust, which contains our hope for life eternal:

"I know that my Redeemer liveth, and that he shall stand at the latter day upon the earth; and though worms destroy this body, yet in my flesh shall I see God. For now is Christ risen from the dead, the firstfruits of them that sleep."

Oh, to know that! To feel that wonderful surety! He looked at the white-robed singer with awe, feeling almost the possibility that she might vanish from their sight into the heavens when this song was over. It never entered his mind but that she felt it all; how else could she sing so to other hearts?

The closing triumphal chorus he heard as in a dream; but he echoed the "blessing and honor, glory and power, for ever and ever," with a glad "Amen" in his heart, keeping in his mind all the while the words, "I know," and resolving that they should be his own someday if ever he could find out how to make them his.

He went out into the dark and wet.

CHAPTER III

The rain had almost ceased; the wind was keener and sharper, and the pavements had become treacherous glass indeed. The throng ahead of him slipped and tottered, and some actually fell. They had to fairly crawl along; but Bradley Benedict heeded none of these things. He was back in the opera house still, face to face with the Man of sorrows; and he scarcely noted which way he was going until a hand was laid upon his shoulder, and a voice, which was altogether too familiar to please him, shouted, "Hello! Which way you goin', and where you bin?"

It was the young man who was to be his roommate, on his way from a cheap theater. He knew the look of the place. He had been to such often before, and taken delight in them; but tonight his heart turned from it with revulsion. He felt as if he had lived years since he entered the opera house that evening.

"I'm going home," he answered his companion shortly; and even as he spoke he felt what a misnomer that word was when applied to the squalid lodging house. He wished he were going home to his mother; and then and there he resolved to go just as soon as he could earn enough to take him.

"H'm!" said the other young man. "Well, you'd better turn around and plod along in the other direction if you expect to get there without going around the world. Come on!" and he turned his unwilling friend about, and, linking his arm in his, walked along by his side.

"Wher've you been?" he asked Benedict presently, as soon as they were out of the worst of the crowd.

"In there," said Benedict, pointing toward the great opera house with a sort of friendly feeling for the building where he had passed through such a strange experience. There was a glow in his heart which he could not understand.

"There!" exclaimed the other in a surprised voice. "You must have a heap of cash. It costs a penny to get in there. What's on tonight? Bernhardt? Let me see. No. Why, it was the oratorio night, wasn't it?" He glanced up at his companion with astonishment and a look almost of respect. "Is that the set you belong to?" he added, as Benedict replied simply by a nod. He had never known exactly what an oratorio was before; but now that he considered the matter, it certainly must have been what he had been listening to.

It was a silent walk the rest of the way to the boarding-house. Benedict's mind was too full of other things to care to talk much, and the young man by his side found he had no conversation ready for the sort of companion who took his amusement at the oratorio *Messiah*. Now and then he glanced curiously at him as they shuffled along over the ice. A keen, strong wind had risen, and afforded sufficient excuse for them to retire behind their coat collars and keep silence.

Bradley Benedict was turning over in his mind this thought: Would this strange, new feeling stay with him, or would it go away and leave his life the same empty void, without purpose or promise, that it had been but a few hours before? He realized now that it had been a bad and worthless life, and wondered at himself for never knowing it before.

Sleep did not come to this young man so soon as to his roommate. The air of the room was breathless; and mingled with the smell of tobacco there was a strong odor of fried onions, lingering probably from the boarding-house supper. His evening in company with refined people, listening to wonderful music, and thinking higher thoughts than had ever entered his mind before, seemed to have quickened his sensibilities to these little things. He felt almost stifled. He arose, went to the window, and threw up the sash. The cold air poured in, and made him shiver; but he threw his coat about his shoulders and looked out. The city was quieting into its after-midnight stillness now; the breeze had blown a small space in the heavy sky for the moon to shine faintly through, which the hurrying clouds were rapidly trying to cover again. One tiny star threw out a few flickering, straggling beams between clouds. The earth looked very dark, save where the lights of the city shone through glass. It was intensely cold. The sky grew black again as the clouds gained a temporary victory over the moon and the one star. Bradley felt alone— alone with God, and "Who shall stand when he appeareth?" came to his mind. Then the moon struggled through the clouds once more, and he thought of the words: "The people that sat in darkness have seen a great light." How many scraps of song he could remember! He felt the same desires which had moved him when he first heard the words —the longing to be able to sing the joyful songs; to feel secure; to have this Friend, this Comforter. Suddenly, as if in answer to his soul's cry, there seemed to come over the wicked city a soft, sweet voice singing the words with tender pathos: "Come unto me, all ye that labor and are heavy laden, and I will give you rest."

He listened until the voice died away on the night, and then in the darkness he bowed his head, and came and found rest.

Mrs. Benedict sat by the remains of a meager fire in the grate of the "parlor," as it was called. The room was deserted by all the boarders now, and she was free to sit here in peace for a few minutes. It was very late, and she was weary—so weary that she had scarcely strength to take her up the stairs to her sleeping room. She had thought earlier in the day that the most delightful thing that could happen to her would be to drop into a bed and stay there, and never have to get up again. She had gone through the day with an almost eager looking forward to the time when she could throw her burdensome tired-out body on the bed, and relax the overstrained muscles for a little time. But here she sat, trying to warm herself from the few weak-looking coals still left in the grate, and gain strength to go up to her room. It had been a more than usually wearisome day. The cook had been undeniably drunk, and not able to do a stroke of work; and the slouchy second girl, who was her only other assistant, had been out late the night before, and had done nothing all day but dawdle about and yawn. One of the young men boarders, whom she had hoped would turn out to be a "permanent," had left that morning; another had departed, leaving a used-up pair of suspenders, and a hat with the crown jammed in, to pay his last month's board. She had decidedly failed in her meek efforts to coax three others into paying something toward past arrears; and the rent collector had called, and told her that he could not wait much longer. Besides all this, she had the neuralgia in one cheek and eye—and her boy was gone away. That was the climax. Her boy! She had thought about it and cried about it until she had no more strength left for either. As she sat looking absently into the coals, where smoldered the stumps of two or three boarders' cigars, a tear trickled weakly down her cheek, scarcely gathering strength enough as it went to fall in a good honest splash in her lap, but spreading itself out in a wet spot among the wrinkles. Her hair was rough and gray; and one lock had escaped from the pin that tried to hold it in a hard knot at the back of her head, and hung now in a discouraged way about her face. The eyes were faded blue, and the skin was so wrinkled you could not guess what the contour of the face might have been in earlier days. She looked a sad picture of despair.

The room itself was a desolate enough place. Mrs. Benedict had been obliged to relax her vigilance for cleanliness during the trials of the past few days; and, as a consequence, the disorder that reigned made it even more Sahara-like than usual. The ashes had spread themselves about on the hearth, and gathered a small collection of toothpicks and cigar stumps. A fine, soft dust was over the mantel, broken here and there by the marks of some boarder's elbow.

There was an emaciated, hollow-chested, haircloth sofa against the wall; a table on the other side of the room, with a faded red-and-black flannel spread, and holding a few *Fireside Companions*. A weary-faced clock on the mantel, a few cane-seat chairs in various stages of dilapidation, and a depressed-looking rocker, completed the furniture of the room. The floor was covered with a large-figured, much faded and darned red-and-green ingrain carpet, helped out in front of door and fireplace by pieces of dreary oilcloth from which the paint had long ago departed. On the walls hung a few family groups and portraits, Mrs. Benedict's marriage certificate, and a cross made of hair flowers, all framed in oval or square black frames.

The marriage certificate occupied the place of honor over the sofa, with a full-length portrait of "Braddie," as she called her son, hanging on one side. He wore baggy plaid trousers that looked full enough for a modern divided skirt, white stockings, a high white collar, and a very short coat, and carried a hat, much too old and large for him, stiffly in one hand. The hair was long and thick, and the face chunky and expressionless, for the photograph was a poor one, and old; but his mother gazed at him, remembered her little boy as he used to be, and sighed a great, deep sigh. Then she turned her tear-dimmed eyes to the picture which hung on the other side. It was a man, presumably, though the picture, which must have been taken long ago, had faded so that little was distinct save some black hair and a coat. The light from the smoky lamp was turned low, however, and there was no bright fire to help out the features. But the lonely heart looking at them knew how the face had looked, and the weak tears gathered and coursed down between their wrinkles thick and fast. It was a hard world, and she was so tired!

A sharp ring of the doorbell broke the stillness of the room, and she looked toward the hall a moment in surprise. Yes, she had locked the door for the night before sitting down. Surely all the boarders were in. The clerk at Mason's came in half an hour ago, and he was always the last one. But she arose mechanically, and went to answer the bell.

She unfastened the lock, and threw back the door, holding the lamp in one hand in front of her eyes, so that she was completely blinded. While the darkness rushed in, and the lamplight staggered out to take its place, she was conscious of somebody standing beside her. It was a strong man like her Braddie. He shut the door, took the lamp from her hand, and then, taking her in his arms, uttered one word: "Mother!"

She was so tired and so glad, and there was a confusion in her mind whether this was really Braddie, or Braddie's father come back to earth again, he seemed so like his father as he held her. She had not been held so for twenty years.

To his old employer Bradley Benedict said the next morning, "I've found God, Mr. Bolton; and I've come home to take care of my mother and prove to you that I'm trying to live a different life, if you'll take me back and try me."

It was two or three years afterward when it was announced that the oratorio *Messiah* would be rendered in the largest church of the place in which the Benedicts lived. Bradley immediately took two tickets, and selected the best seats the house afforded. Then he said, "Mother, the oratorio *Messiah* is to be here next week, and I want you to hear it. It is what saved me, and brought me home to begin life over again."

And Mrs. Benedict, not in the least knowing what

an oratorio was, but glad to please "her Braddie," donned her plain black silk, and combed her white hair to its smoothest, and went. She sat and watched her tall boy proudly through the whole evening, and told him at the close it was a nice concert, as good as any she and his father ever went to. But of the music she heard little, and she wondered in her heart what it could possibly be in that singing which had anything to do with Bradley's coming home.

Things have changed since Bradley Benedict came home that night. The boarders are gone, and the family has moved to a small, cozy house. The old furniture has given place to bright, cheery belongings, and Mrs. Benedict is renewing her youth under the loving care of her son.

Oh, ye disciples of Fashion and Art, as I passed by and beheld your devotions, I found an altar, in this oratorio *Messiah*, set up by you "To the Unknown God." Whom therefore ye ignorantly worship, him could this unlearned young man declare unto you. For God, "that made the world and all things therein, and hath made of one blood all nations for to dwell on all the face of the earth, and hath determined the times before appointed, and the bounds of their habitation; that they should seek the Lord, if haply they might feel after him, and find him, though he be not far from every one of us."

UNDER THE
WINDOW

HE little bronze clock on the shelf over the fireplace chimed out seven, and then took up its next hour's work of counting out the seconds to the sleeping cat on the hearth. The room was all alone, and very still, having a quiet time by itself. The fire winked and blinked at the lamp, and the lamp beamed brightly back from under its homemade shade of rose-colored tissue paper and cardboard. The carpet, a neat ingrain, looked as if it knew its place and what was expected of it—namely, to look prettier than it really was, to wear long and not show dirt—and it would not presume upon its privileges even when the mistress was out. The sofa was wide, deep, and comfortable, made of a dry-goods box, with a wide board nailed on for a back, and the whole deftly padded and covered with an old crimson shawl, with fringes too shabby to be used any longer as an outside wrap.

There were curtains too. You wouldn't have had

them in your room. They were nothing but cheesecloth with rows of threads pulled and tied; but they
were cheap, and gave a pretty air of grace and home-
liness to the room. Besides, they were held back
from the windows by broad yellow satin ribbons. To
be sure, the ribbons were only old pink ones, washed
and dyed with diamond dye; but they were yellow,
and added a dainty touch to the plainness of other
things.

There was a small table with a red cover, which
held the lamp; two wooden chairs, a little rocker
covered with cretonne, and a stool near the hearth.
Above the table was a little shelf with a Bible and
a few other books.

The only really elegant things in the room were
the bronze clock and two delicate vases of Parian
marble; but these were presents from some former
little pupils of the mistress, and, as such, occupied
the place of honor—the broad shelf over the wide,
old-fashioned fireplace. But they seemed to have
made friends with the ingrain carpet, the homemade
sofa, and the cheesecloth curtains, and to feel quite
as much at home with the yellow ribbons as though
the latter had been real and new, not old and dyed.
There were a few pictures and bright cards that
smiled down from the walls—and the room kept
very still and waited, all alone. Now and again the
white cat stirred in his sleep, opened one eye up at
the clock, as though he had just heard it strike those
seven clear strokes, pushed his forepaws slowly,
tremblingly forward, in the luxury of a stretch,
opened his mouth to its utmost extent, then turned

over to cuddle down again, one paw over his nose, and a contented smile on his pink cat mouth.

There were two windows in the room, one looking out on the little strip of ground between the house and the street, the other opening to a sort of lane or alley; and this window was down from the top several inches, for the mistress had ideas on ventilation. The wind came in and stirred the curtains, even waving the least mite the white fur on the end of the cat's tail; but the cat was used to drafts, and did not mind. He only gave his ear a little nervous jerk, as if he fancied it were summer, and a fly were biting him; though he knew better if he had only stopped to think, for here was the fire, and outside was the snow blowing, and the breath of air that had touched his tail was decidedly cold. There were other reasons too. His mistress had not taken that pile of books and started off to school for three whole days. By that he knew it was the winter vacation. Then, had not old Mr. and Mrs. Updike, from whom he and his mistress rented their rooms, gone away that very morning to spend the holidays with their daughter Hepzibah? The cat and his mistress were alone in the house, except for Peter Kelly, who was probably at that moment sitting in his room over the kitchen, his chair tilted back against the wall, and looking straight at the spluttering flame of his candle.

And why didn't his mistress go away to spend the holidays, and not stay all the happy Christmastide shut up in her little room with her cat? Well, in the first place, she couldn't afford to go away. She was just a poor little schoolteacher, with a very small

salary, barely enough to support herself and her cat;
for a cat she would have, she said, if she had to go
without something herself. Second, she couldn't
leave her cat. Who would take care of it? Not Mrs.
Updike, for she hated cats; and besides, she was not
at home. Third, she had nowhere to go; and so she
stayed at home. She had told the white cat only a few
days ago that she was all alone in the world, and had
dropped a bright tear on his pink ear, and he had
twitched his head in surprise. She was no worse off
in that respect than he was, and he was contented.
He saw no further need for anyone in the world besides himself and her, except, perhaps, the milkman.

But at that moment the front door opened and
closed with a bang: there was a sound of stamping
and brushing in the hall; then the mistress entered,
and the room seemed to smile and brighten to re-
ceive her. Bright brown eyes, golden brown hair,
straight nose, cheeks glowing with the cold and exercise, straight eyebrows, and small brown hands—
that is Polly Bronson. She wore a dark-blue flannel
dress, a black jersey coat, black mittens, and a little
black crocheted cap with balls on the top. The snowflakes glistened over all. She shook them gaily off,
laid her parcels on the table, and went to hang up her
things in the small bedroom adjoining. Coming back,
she seated herself on the little stool, and proceeded
to poke the fire, making it blaze up brightly.

"Come here, Abbott," she said merrily, "while I
tell you the news."

The cat slowly arose, humped his back up high,
curled his tail into an impossible position, stuck out

each particular hair of his white coat, until he looked like a porcupine, and yawned. Then he closed one eye, and went and rubbed his head sideways against Polly's foot.

"Oh, you lazy Abbott, wake up!" cried Polly, as she caught him in her arms and shook him gently.

"Listen, Abbott! I've something nice to tell you. Tomorrow is Christmas, you know."

Abbott gravely winked. Polly was in the habit of telling her plans to him; and he was a good listener, always agreeing with her.

"Well, now, if you and I were rich, Abbott, we would give each other presents, beautiful presents. People do that at Christmas; did you know it?"

The cat looked inquiringly at her with his bright green eyes. Polly's face was a picture of mock gravity as she said, "I wish I had a present to give you, my poor little cat, but I am so sorry I have none." The cat looked disappointed. "But you shall have an extra saucer of milk tomorrow for breakfast." The cat brightened. "And, Abbott, we'll have a party, you and I, and we'll invite Susie and Mamie Bryce, and Joey Wilkes, and little lame Tim. They are poor little children, Abbott, without any Christmas at all; and you must be a good cat, and play with them, and not go to sleep on the hearth for the whole evening."

Abbott uttered a feeble "Meow!" as protest; but Polly went on:

"We can't have a turkey, it costs too much. Abbott, did you know they always have turkey on Christmas? Yes, and cranberries; but you wouldn't

like those: they're sour. We'll have baked beans—
they're cheap, you know, and you like them—and an
Indian pudding, all baked very nice and brown, with
plenty of big, fat raisins in it. And, Abbott,
some oysters! Yes, really, just for once. They won't
cost much; and you shall have two all to yourself,
perhaps three!"

Abbott purred contentedly and settled himself in
her lap for another nap; but a gust of air from the
window sent Polly in haste to close the forgotten
shutters, and the cat concluded it was best to go back
to the hearth.

Just as those seven strokes had sounded from
Polly's bronze clock, a young man stood on the snowy
pavement not many blocks away, hands in his
pockets, wondering how he should spend Christmas
Eve. He was all alone in the city, too, with not even
a cat to cheer him. He had acquaintances, of course
—a few—but what were they on Christmas Eve?
Some were out of town; and some were in their
homes at merrymakings of their own, to which they
had not even thought to invite him. He told himself
he wouldn't have gone if they had; and he ground his
heels into the hard snow, and thought of his mother's
cheerful kitchen, with its wide old fireplace and
pleasant Christmas odors, the dear father and
mother and brother and little sister, even the cat
who blinkingly thought over her vanished youth,
gazing into the glowing fire. How their faces would
brighten if he could walk in upon them now! Indeed,
he must stop such thoughts as these. He told himself
that he wasn't a baby, to expect always to be at

home for Christmas, and to hang up his stocking.

But it was cold, and he could not stand there much longer. Should he go back to his office? No. He had endured that as long as he could for that evening; for John Brewer and his smiling wife, who rented the room just back of his, were having a little tea-drinking, and the peals of merry laughter which came from there every few minutes did not tend to make the young man feel less lonely. He dismissed as quickly the idea that he should go to his dingy little room in the grim boarding-house on High Street. He would call on the gentleman who had left his card that day at the office, with the message that he had some important business matters to talk over with him at his earliest convenience. This would be as good a time as any to call; and the gentleman would be likely to be in his room, as he was a stranger in town. He turned and walked down the little alley, the nearest road to Park Avenue, the Grand Hotel, and the stranger.

Halfway down the alley he discovered he could not recall the name of the man, for he had only glanced at the card hastily as it lay on his table. He fumbled in his pocket for it, so that he might consult it at the next lamp post; but a nearer opportunity offered itself in the shape of Polly Bronson's bright little side window, and he stepped up to it as Polly entered with her bundles. He had just found the right card when he heard the cheery voice calling: "Abbott, come here!" Of course he looked up; and of course, having seen and heard so much, it was not in nature for a lonely man to be in haste to tramp off to make a business call on a stranger. He saw in that fireplace a little of the home cheer of his mother's hearth; he saw in the white cat's face something of the thoughtfulness of the home cat; he saw in the young girl—well, I'm not sure what he saw in her; you'll have to ask him. She was just Polly, you know; something new and bright and beautiful.

Yes, he stood and watched the pretty tableau enacted before him. He let his eyes rove around the little room, and he called it pretty! He did not know the curtains were cheesecloth and the ribbons dyed. He heard every word that Polly said, too—for you remember the window was down from the top— from the presents down to the Indian pudding and the oysters, and wished with all his heart that he was poor little Tim, or somebody who could be invited to that party. Listening? He never thought of such a thing. Indeed, he did not think of anything but the interesting picture and the story that had unfolded itself right before his eyes.

He did recover his senses sufficiently to remember that he was not invisible when Polly came toward the window, and he stepped back into the shadow. There was a sort of blank when the shutters were closed and the cheery room was shut from his view. He did not feel in the least like making that call now. It was scarcely five minutes, and yet he felt that he had some new friends in the city. He had a feeling of pity for the lonely girl; and so in thinking of others, lost sight of his own loneliness.

He very soon discovered that he was standing in a snowbank. Stamping himself out of it, he took his way mechanically to the Grand Hotel, thinking, meanwhile, of what he had seen, reading between the lines of the bit of a story he had been allowed to hear. He was relieved to find that the gentleman of whom he was in search was not in, and he went home with a pleasant little plan taking shape in his brain. It was too bad that the little girl should not have any Christmas present, he thought. What if he should send her one himself? It did not seem exactly the right thing, to send an anonymous present to a young lady who had never seen him; but there certainly could be no harm in sending one to a cat. Nobody ever heard of there being any harm in that.

Very early on Christmas morning, when few in the city were stirring, only the milk wagon or the baker's cart rattling over the frosty stones of the street, and now and then a sleepy clerk taking down shutters and opening doors, he was walking with a brisk step toward a flower store kept by a little old lady of whom he had once or twice bought flowers to send to his mother. He bought a wealth of roses this morning—great yellow Maréchal Niels, delicate Safranas only halfway open, and buds of Bon Silines with their wonderful perfume. Then he selected a satin ribbon of faint green tinge for the old lady to fasten them together with, and the whole was put in the prettiest white basket, well wrapped in cotton and white tissue paper, and a card fastened to the handle: "For my friend Abbott, a very Merry Christmas."

Then the young man walked with a smiling face, and calmly deposited the basket on Mr. Samuel Updike's front doorstep and retreated, wishing much that he dared remain and watch the outcome. Polly, who was allowing herself nice long holiday sleeps, slept on with one brown hand under a rosy cheek, and never dreamed that there was a something on her doorstep that would fill her with delight and wonder all that day, and for many days after. But Abbott must have heard a noise; for he shivered a little, opened one eye at the dying fire, wondered why his mistress did not get up, then rolled to the edge of the rug nearest the fire, and went to sleep again.

Polly did wake up by and by, made up the fire, and got breakfast. After breakfast Abbott sat on the hearth licking his whiskers and washing his paws, and thinking how very nice it was to have an extra saucer of milk, while Polly brushed up the room, opened the windows, and stood the hall door and the front door wide open. There was the basket! Polly's exclamation brought Abbott to the door. He thought it must be another milkman, and he always went to meet the milkman, unless it rained. He sniffed around the basket, and looked as curious as his mistress while she read the card aloud.

"Why, Abbott! It's a Christmas present for you! But who sent it? and what is it? Where did you get a friend that I don't know about? It certainly isn't Mr. or Mrs. Updike, or Peter Kelly, or the milkman; and I'm sure I don't know who else knows you. O Abbott, I wish you could talk!"

Abbott tried to let her know by eyes and ears, as

well as a cat can, that if he could talk he could give her no information on the subject.

"Let's open it, Abbott."

Thereupon the cat and basket were transferred to the sofa. Amid many exclamations the roses came to light, filling the little room with their elegant fragrance. Polly caught the cat up, and kissed the very tip of his pink ear. It was dreadful, I know; but then Polly was very happy, and she had no one else to kiss.

"You dear cat! You shall invite your friend to the party, so you shall, if you will give the invitation."

Perhaps Abbott understood, for he went to the door and sat looking out. Presently he walked down the steps and over the snowy path, putting each paw down carefully, lest it might get too much mixed with the snow. When he reached the gate he gave one spring to the top of the gatepost, and paused a moment, looking up and down the street, and then, seeming to decide which way he would go, sprang down, and trotted off as though he had business that would require haste.

Polly talked to everything that morning while she worked. She called to Abbott at the door that he should wear the green ribbon to the party; and he looked back and winked assent as he put the first velvet paw into the snow. She told the vases that they were dear, beautiful things, and she was glad at last that there was something for them to hold, and she hoped they would keep them very carefully a long time. Polly worked fast, and was soon ready to go out to do her marketing and give her invitations. She decided to have her party at night; because Mamie Bryce had to go down on Sycamore Street and take care of Mrs. Dobell's baby, while Mrs. Dobell went to a dinner party, and she could not get back until four o'clock. So Polly told them all to come at five; and their eyes shone brightly as they promised.

It was beginning to grow dark. Little flurries of snow filled the air. The young man—Porter Mason was his name—hurried along the street, hands in his pockets, collar turned up, and hat drawn over his eyes. He had been away off to the other end of the city on some good errand or other; was cold and tired and hungry, and it was still a long walk home. He was wondering if he should dare to venture around to that alley again when it grew quite dark; if the window blinds would be open; if he should see the roses anywhere; and if the party would be over. In a lull between the chime of sleighbells came a faint "Meow!" and he looked sharply around. The "Meow-ow-ow-ow!" came more distinctly now; and soon just ahead of him he spied a weary white form moving dejectedly through the fast-falling snow. He stooped and picked it up, brushing the snow off, and holding it up to the light of a near street lamp.

"I believe you are the very cat!" he said, speaking aloud. "But how in the world did you get here? Is your name Abbott?"

"Meow!" said the cat.

"All right, then; you're my friend. Jump right in

here and make yourself comfortable." He opened his big overcoat, and tucked the cat snugly in. "I shouldn't wonder if I had my invitation, after all," he told himself as he went on briskly.

Within Polly Bronson's cherry room all was not as serene as might have been. The little party had assembled, and were sitting on the edges of their chairs, undergoing the first embarrassment of arrival; but there was a shadow besides embarrassment over them. The trouble was that two of them were missing. The one was the guest little Tim, and the other was the host himself, Abbott. Tim could not come, because his father was too drunk to carry him, and the streets were too slippery to trust him with his little crutch. His mother would have brought him, for it was his first bit of pleasure for many a day; but she, poor soul, was on her back, scarcely able to wait upon herself. Nobody knew what had become of Abbott.

That is the way matters stood when Porter Mason rang the bell of the Updike house, which so startled Susie and Mamie Bryce and Joey Wilkes that they all huddled together on one chair, like so many frightened peas in a pan when the pan is suddenly tipped up. Mr. Mason had gone straight to the little lane side window, and found the shutters closed. Now what should he do? Would it be safe to risk a peep in at the front window? Suppose the real Abbott were inside, snug and warm by the fire? How foolish he would feel appearing at the door of a strange young lady, in the dark of a snowy night, and saying,

"Have you lost a cat, madam?" without giving a reason for supposing that she had a cat.

He stood in the snowbank again and thought, and kitty purred under his warm coat. He might say that he had once, when passing, seen a cat there. It wasn't in the least likely that the young lady would question him as to the circumstances under which he had seen the cat, and she would in all probability suppose him to have seen it on the doorstep. He concluded to risk this statement, and so boldly rang the bell.

Polly hurried to the door. She was not in the habit of having evening callers. The door, being opened, let in such a whirlwind of snowflakes that Polly could distinguish nothing in the gathering darkness save the tall form of a man powdered with snow from head to foot. He was taking off his hat and saying in a pleasant voice, "Have you lost a cat?" As he said it he cast an anxious glance through the half-open door to the glowing fireplace, and was relieved to see no cat there.

"Oh, yes!" her senses having come back to her. "Won't you come in? Do you know where he is?"

"I found one on the street; and, remembering to have seen one at this house, I brought it here."

He was unbuttoning his coat now, and handed Abbott, warm and somewhat damp, to his mistress.

"Oh, thank you so much!" she said as she took him. "I'm so glad to get him back. I was troubled about him when it began to snow so hard. I was afraid he was lost."

She paused and looked up. Abbott's rescuer looked very cold and blue as he stood there in the chilly hall. Perhaps he had come out of his way to bring the cat, she thought. He had a chilly feeling at his heart too; he began to think that it was time he should say, "You're quite welcome; good-evening," and bow himself out, and go to his cold, dingy room. He seemed to see the supper to which he would presently be called, remnants of the departed dinner. He glanced again into the cheery room, and then was about to bow his good-evening, when Polly's voice interrupted—"Won't you come in to the fire and get warm? You must be very cold."

Polly never thought of being afraid to ask a stranger in. She was never afraid of anything. She was twenty-two, and had taken care of herself for nearly five years, and she felt as if nothing in the world could harm her. Then there were the children; and she had a secure sense of Peter Kelly in his back chamber over the kitchen. Besides, had not this stranger done her a kindness; and did she not owe something to him? And he had kind eyes, and a gentle hand with the kitten. There are always reasons enough when a bright girl does anything.

But she was surprised when, instead of saying, "No, I thank you," he hesitated, and said, "May I?"

Polly, with glowing cheeks, ushered her caller into the bright room, and seated him in the rocking chair, hardly knowing what to make of him, or what to do with him when she got him there. But the children helped her with their gleeful exclamations over the lost-and-found cat. Abbott, however, slipped from their caressing hands, and retired to the hearth to bathe. He was a neat cat, and did not like to appear before company with his white coat all stiff and rough.

"Where did you say you found him?" questioned Polly. Mr. Mason did not say, but launched into a full description of Abbott's pitiful cries and forlorn appearance, until the question was forgotten in a merry round of laughter, in which Polly joined, in spite of herself, although she had determined to be very dignified.

"Oh!" cried Susie when the laughter had somewhat subsided, "wouldn't we be having just a lovely time if Tim were only here."

"Yes," said Mamie, the laughter all sobered out of her face. "He stood at the top of the stairs, and cried and cried when we came down." And even stout little Joey Wilkes said it was "just too awful mean for anything."

"And who is Tim?" asked the strange visitor, as soon as there was any chance for him to speak.

The children burst into full explanation of the case, all together of course, and it was some time before he could understand. Even then he was left in doubt as to whether more sorrow had been felt for Abbott, or for little Tim with his drunken father.

He arose at last, and turned to Polly, "Having brought back one of the missing guests, it becomes needful that I should complete my good work, and bring the other. It would be a pity to have the perfection of this party spoiled by the shadow of an absent guest. Can you direct me where to find this boy?"

He buttoned up his coat, and the children danced for joy and clapped their hands, crying, "Goody, goody!"

Polly's face was beaming all over with a pleased surprise; but she tried to draw up her slipping cloak of dignity, and say, "Oh, no! You really must not go to that trouble for us this stormy night."

Mr. Mason, however, would listen to no such talk, and obtained the desired information. He turned to go, then stopped, fumbling in his pockets; but as no card was to be found, he produced a bit of folded pasteboard, saying, "I have no card with me, but will this do as well? My name is the fourth one on the list of leaders, and when I come back we'll get Tim to introduce us."

The well-known letters "Y. P. S. C. E." met her eyes from the cover of the card, and below, "Hartford Square Church." A little smile played over her face. She need not be quite so careful now that she knew so much about him. Turning to the next page, she ran over the list of leaders and their subjects, especially the fourth one. She laid the card on the shelf, and went back to her oil stove. The pudding was just taking on the last delicate shades of brown, and needed watching. She hastened to set her table, putting one more plate on; for, she told herself, she supposed that young man must be invited to supper, after he had taken so much trouble for them. Then she thought of Peter Kelly.

Now, Peter was of that nondescript age when one

does not know what to call him. It seemed strange to designate him as a young man; and yet he was not a boy, nor an old man, nor even a middle-aged man. Yes, he certainly must be a young man; but it seemed so odd to call him that. He had colorless hair and expressionless eyes. The world had not used him badly; indeed, it had not used him much at all either way, and he had not used it; therefore he had no identity with it. Peter was connected with the Hartford Square Church; that is, he swept the floors and looked after the rooms—was, in short, janitor. Remembering this, she filled a plate with some baked beans and one slice of the delicate toast that stood ready for the hot oysters, and pouring a cup of steaming coffee, she went with swift steps to the back chamber, and knocked.

The front legs of Peter's chair came to the floor with a bang, and he sat with his mouth wide open, staring at the door, after giving his gruff, "Come in."

Polly entered, setting down her burden and saying rapidly, "I've brought you some of my baked beans; they're hot, and I thought you might like them, Peter."

She never knew what sort of thanks he stammered out. She was busy thinking how she should put her question.

"Peter, do you know any one at the Hartford Square Church by the name of Mason?"

This was as near the name as she would come. She would not have dared so much if he had been like some people; but talking to Peter was much like talking to Abbott. He would never put two and two together, or wonder why she had asked such a question.

"Wal, yas," said Peter, diverted from his astonishment; "thar's two on 'em. Thar's John—he's a carpenter; an' thar's Porter—he's a law'er. I reckon you mean him. Is he tall an' han'some? great big eyes an' black hair, an' allus a good word said jes' so's to help most?"

"I think he must be the gentleman I have met," said Polly demurely.

"Wal, he's a mighty nice feller; give me a ticket to a church supper th' other evenin'. He's awful smart, too, an' good. They do say he wouldn't have nothin' to do with a case Judge Granger give him, cause he thought it wa'n't right; an' he ain't rich, neither. But you'd just ought to hear him pray! Thar's allus a big meetin' up to the C. E. when he leads."

Polly had all the information she wanted now, and made haste to get away, amid a shower of rough thanks from Peter. She went gleefully to her room, and found the children so busy with a picture book that they had scarcely noticed her absence. So she knelt by the fireplace and stroked Abbott. Now that he was dry and smooth, Polly tied the rich green ribbon around his neck, much to the delight of the children. She stuck a Safrana bud in the bow, and set him upon the stool. There he sat, the long ends of shining satin reaching to his toes, holding his chin very high, either from the choking sensation of the broad ribbon, or pride in his rich apparel; probably pride, for he seemed quite contented, and sat purring at the children with his eyes half closed.

Porter Mason, with happy Tim mounted on his shoulder, came to a sudden halt before a large fruit store.

"Tim, would you like to take Miss Bronson a Christmas present?" he asked.

They had been talking of her all the way along, and Tim had said he loved her next best to his mother in all the world. They were pretty well acquainted by this time, so Tim answered, "You just bet! Wouldn't I, though?"

"All right. We'll go in here, and you shall choose what it shall be."

It almost took Tim's breath away to see so many good things together; but after grave consideration he pointed to a box of great white California grapes. You might have thought Mr. Mason extravagant for a man who "wasn't rich" if you'd heard his order to the clerk; but little Tim was very happy, and his companion looked none the less so.

"Well, Miss Bronson," said Mr. Mason, after they were fairly in, and Tim had presented his gift, "is the courier to be allowed to stay to the party, or must I go outside and paw the pavement until my services are needed again? Or I might go off and come back at a certain hour?"

What could Polly do but give him a gracious invitation?

So he took his coat and hat to the hall, and made himself quite at home, telling the children stories, and giving them such a wonderful time, while Polly cooked the oysters, that they forgot how hungry they were. They had a great time getting seated at the table. Polly actually ventured to borrow four of Mrs. Updike's best splint-bottomed kitchen chairs, and they all went after them except Tim and Abbott, who sat and smiled at one another while they were gone. But they were seated at last, and then came a moment Polly was not altogether prepared for. She had meant to ask a blessing. She always did when by herself, and she wanted not to leave God out before these children, and on Christmas night; but here was this stranger. Could she ask him?

Polly's daring spirit came uppermost. She looked up and said quietly, "Will you ask a blessing?"

Then what a light of pleasure and surprise rushed into the eyes that met hers. He bowed his head, and his few earnest, clear-spoken words to God astonished the children more than his stories had done. They were evidently not used to this.

While Polly was pouring out coffee, Mr. Mason questioned the children, and found they knew almost nothing at all about Christmas; so he promised to tell them the true story of it after tea, and they gave themselves up to the delights of their plates.

"Miss Bronson promised to sing some too," said Susie Bryce, with her mouth full of beans. Now, Polly did not intend to keep that promise, with the stranger there to listen; so she passed him the sugar, and asked Tim if he would have some more oysters. The Indian pudding was hailed with joy, and pronounced by Mr. Mason "just as good as his mother's." Then they finished off with some of those luscious grapes. They were such a treat to Polly, and to the children something wonderful. Abbott had his three oysters, and enjoyed them as much as anybody.

After supper, while Polly was clearing off the table, the children had their story. Polly, going about her work very softly, that she might lose none of it, told herself that she did not wonder that they liked to come to meeting when he led, if he talked like that. When she had finished she sat down very quietly, but the story was just closing, and Mr. Mason turned to her and said, "Now may we have the song, Miss Bronson?"

Polly did not wish, did not intend, to sing to him. She had "No" written all over her pretty, flushed face, despite the children's eager pleadings, until Mr. Mason said, "I think I shall have to go out and stand in the snow, after all, for I don't want the children to lose their pleasure because of me."

Polly somehow had to sing then; and though her voice trembled some, it was sweet and clear as she sang:

Little stars that twinkle in the heavens blue,
I have often wondered if you ever knew
How there rose one like you, leading wise old men
From the east, through Judah, down to Bethlehem?

Did you watch the Savior all those years of strife?
Did you know for sinners, how he gave his life?
Little stars that twinkle in the heavens blue,
All you saw of Jesus, how I wish I knew.

Then Polly stopped; and she would not sing again for all their coaxing, for she had been too conscious of those eyes that had watched her so closely during the singing to try again. So she started some games, and they had a frolic until the clock on the mantel warned them that it was getting late, and Mr. Mason told little Tim it was time for his carriage to take him home. The children sighed that the happy time was over. Tim was given some of the grapes and a rosebud or two for his sick mother. Polly bundled him up, and gave each of the children a rose, and then they were ready to go.

Mr. Mason gravely walked up to the fire, where weary Abbott, in spite of his elegance, had succumbed to the warmth and the remembrance of a delicious supper, and had gone to sleep. But he was a polite cat, and as Mr. Mason came up, let him shake hands, or paws, with him.

Tim was mounted once more on his shoulder; Polly's hand was taken for just a second, and—"I have enjoyed it all so much; might I come again soon, and make a party call?"

Of course she had to say yes; and then, with Susie and Mamie just behind, and Joey Wilkes scudding on ahead, they started out into the snow, and the party was ended.

Yes, he came very soon to make the call; and then he wanted to come again and again, until it grew to be a settled thing for him to run in once or twice a week with a bit of a poem for her to read, or a book to talk over. In those days she had roses sent to her, instead of to her cat; she was taken out to Sunday evening meetings quite often, and now and then to a concert or a lecture. Abbott was left at home, which he did not like after having been alone all day. As spring came on there were violets and anemones, and once a lovely ride to the woods on a Saturday afternoon. Then a note came from the mother of a former pupil, saying that her little daughter was very sick, could not live long, and wanted to have her dear Miss Bronson with her, which the doctor said would help. Would she come to them as soon as possible?

Polly sighed, packed away her bronze clock and marble vases, packed up the things she must take with her, waited a whole day hoping somebody would call—then gave Abbott into the keeping of a quaint new neighbor. She gave special directions to Mrs. Updike to say to whomever called that she had been summoned to a sick friend and would probably be back soon, and went.

It was not a long journey, fifty miles or so, and the little pupil was very glad to see her. She grew no better as the days went by. It soon became evident that Polly could not be spared, for Bessie was not happy a moment unless her teacher was by her side. The mother was an invalid herself, who made her little girl worse by her melancholy speeches; so, although Polly was longing to be at home, she did not feel as if she ought to go. She stayed, and Bessie grew day by day weaker, but lingered on until the summer was drawing near its close, and the winter school term was about to begin; then she slipped into heaven, leaving Polly, who had made the way bright for her, almost worn out with loss of sleep and confinement to the sick room. She hurried home to begin school life again. She unpacked the clock and vases, and reestablished Abbott, who walked round and round her, purring and rubbing his head against her, trying as best he could to tell that he did not like boarding, and was glad to be at home again. When Polly received the key of her room, and asked if there had been anyone to call, she gained only a sentence about a tall man who 'kep' a coming' "; and that was all the news of home she had.

Porter Mason had been very lonely after Polly left. He had called many times to see her; but Mrs. Updike never knew her address, and now, just as Polly had come home, he had been called away on business. When he finally reached home he found such a quantity of matters awaiting his attention that he had no time to think of doing anything for pleasure. So it happened that Polly had been at home for three weeks without once having seen Mr. Mason.

One evening she took Abbott in her arms and went to the front door. The air was chilly and hazy, as late September is apt to be. The stars were not nearly as bright as usual. They had no sparkle. They looked as if they had all gone away to spend the evening, and had left only a dim light in the window. It was lonesome and cold. She shivered, and dropped a few tears on Abbott's thick coat. She did not hear the brisk steps coming down the street as she went in and shut the door; but they came on, right to Polly's bright little window, which had been so dark for many a day when those same steps had sounded down the street. And when Mr. Mason came in he took Polly's two hands in his own and held them— Abbott had his back turned, looking into the fire—

and when he had made her quite comfortable on the sofa, he sat down beside her, and told her something; but we must not hear it. If you have heard such words yourself, you understand; if you have not, wait until your turn comes to know.

What did Polly say? Why, she said it to Mr. Mason; and no one heard, not even Abbott, for he was asleep, and Mr. Mason never told.

They both went to the cheerful home among the hills to spend their next holidays, and make glad the hearts of the dear father and mother and brother and little sister and the other cat. Abbott, much to his disgust, was obliged to spend his holidays with the quaint little neighbor; and when his mistress came back she took him to another part of the town to live, where the familiar objects were all about him. There was a rug that he always lay on, crocheted out of strips of silk; and the yellow stripes were the yellow ribbons that used to hold back the cheesecloth curtains. He thought it rather queer that Polly never went to school anymore, and that the tall stranger stayed all the time now; but he liked him, and so it was all right. He had all the beefsteak and milk and oysters he wanted, and could wear a green ribbon and rosebuds any day if he chose—so he told the cats of the neighborhood.

And so the old room has seen the story; has helped it along, as it has helped many before, and stands again waiting, all alone, except for the big black spider who is hanging her delicate draperies in all the corners. It waits for someone to enter and bring life and beauty to it again.